PUFFIN BOOKS

TEACHER'S PET

I adopted my owner, Andrew Cope, when he visited the RSPCA. He seemed a nice enough chap. Perhaps not the brightest. But clean. Well-mannered. All his own teeth. And best of all, I knew I'd be able to train him. The plan was to convince him he was clever and I was just a mutt. I persuaded him to write some books about me. And now he chauffeurs me to schools and book festivals. I have my own 'Spy Dog' engraved dog bowl, diamond-encrusted collar and Harrod's basket (with luxury feather pillow). I live a life of total relaxation and luxury. While Andrew Cope works his socks off. I ask you, reader, who do you think is the clever one?

If you want Lara or her puppy to visit your school, please email her at lara@artofbrilliance.co.uk. They'll probably have to bring Andrew Cope along too, but don't let that put you off. Or you can find out more about the Spy Dog and Spy Pups books online at *www.spydog451.co.uk*, where there are pictures, videos and competitions too!

SPY DOG
TEACHER'S PET

ANDREW COPE

Illustrated by James de la Rue

PUFFIN

PUFFIN BOOKS

Published by the Penguin Group
Penguin Books Ltd, 80 Strand, London WC2R ORL, England
Penguin Group (USA) Inc., 375 Hudson Street, New York, New York 10014, USA
Penguin Group (Canada), 90 Eglinton Avenue East, Suite 700, Toronto, Ontario, Canada M4P 2Y3
(a division of Pearson Penguin Canada Inc.)
Penguin Ireland, 25 St Stephen's Green, Dublin 2, Ireland (a division of Penguin Books Ltd)
Penguin Group (Australia), 707 Collins Street, Melbourne, Victoria 3008, Australia
(a division of Pearson Australia Group Pty Ltd)
Penguin Books India Pvt Ltd, 11 Community Centre, Panchsheel Park, New Delhi – 110 017, India
Penguin Group (NZ), 67 Apollo Drive, Rosedale, Auckland 0632, New Zealand
(a division of Pearson New Zealand Ltd)
Penguin Books (South Africa) (Pty) Ltd, Block D, Rosebank Office Park, 181 Jan Smuts Avenue,
Parktown North, Gauteng 2193, South Africa

Penguin Books Ltd, Registered Offices: 80 Strand, London WC2R ORL, England

puffinbooks.com

First published 2010
This edition published 2012
001

Text copyright © Andrew Cope and Stella Maidment, 2010
Illustrations copyright © James de la Rue, 2010
All rights reserved

The moral right of the author and illustrator has been asserted

Set in Bembo
Typeset by Palimpsest Book Production Limited, Falkirk, Stirlingshire
Printed in Great Britain by Clays Ltd, St Ives plc

British Library Cataloguing in Publication Data
A CIP catalogue record for this book is available from the British Library

ISBN: 978-0-141-34559-8

www.greenpenguin.co.uk

Penguin Books is committed to a sustainable
future for our business, our readers and our planet.
This book is made from Forest Stewardship
Council™ certified paper.

MIX
Paper from
responsible sources
FSC
www.fsc.org
FSC™ C018179

ALWAYS LEARNING   **PEARSON**

For everyone who goes to school each day – children, teachers, head teachers, dinner ladies and especially Isabel, Alfie, Leo, Teddy and Charlie

Contents

1. Daylight Robbery

The afternoon air was heavy and still. The sun burnt down relentlessly and, high above the drowsy village, a plane's white vapour trail crept silently across the sky. There was nothing and no one about.

No one saw the car stop outside the house, or the two men looking quickly from side to side and pulling up their hoods. No one heard the smash of glass as the back window was struck with a single hammer blow, and no one witnessed the leather-gloved hand reach in and turn the catch.

Inside the house the thieves moved quickly through the rooms, turning over cushions, opening cupboards, pulling out drawers. They looked in the fridge and the washing machine. They threw books out of bookcases and tipped

clothes out of the laundry basket. They even got a stepladder and went up in the loft.

They ignored the flat-screen television and

the laptop. They paid no attention to the camera or the electric guitar. They certainly weren't interested in the exercise books piled up on the table waiting to be marked – they just scattered them over the floor as they hurried past.

The men took pictures off the walls and hurled them on the floor. They sliced open the sofa and armchair. They ripped up the carpet and prised open a loose floorboard, revealing the wires and pipes underneath. Then, as the clock on the microwave flashed to 15.15, they pushed down their hoods, opened the front door, pocketed their gloves and were gone.

No one saw or heard a thing, but when Mr Thompson came home from school that afternoon he certainly got a nasty surprise.

2. The Email

A mile or so away across the village, a black and white dog about the size of a Labrador, with one ear that flopped down and another that stuck up, was relaxing in a deckchair. She had finished her sudoku puzzle and was lying back with her eyes closed, enjoying the sun.

Lara was thinking what a lucky dog she was to have such a great home with Mr and Mrs Cook and their three children Ben, Sophie and Ollie.

A butterfly landed on her long, doggie nose and, as she brushed it carefully away, she thought about the old days when her name was just Agent GM451 and her official job title was LARA – Licensed Assault and Rescue Animal.

Life in the Secret Service was certainly exciting, thought Lara, *but it was pretty scary sometimes too*.

Unconsciously she moved her paw to touch the perfectly round bullet hole in her sticking-up ear. That was a souvenir of one of her more dangerous missions. *Things certainly got a bit hairy then*. It was on that assignment that Lara was forced to pose as an ordinary dog, and then got herself adopted by the Cooks.

That was the best thing I ever did, thought Lara. *It was fun being a secret agent and I liked catching all those baddies, but I'd rather be part of a normal family*.

Just then she heard some excited woofs from the end of the garden. Lara peered through her sunglasses at her two lively pups, Spud and

Star. They were playing a very splashy game of tug-of-war with the garden hose.

'Calm down, you two!' she woofed, trying to sound stern. 'You're meant to be watering the plants, not each other!'

No, I'm very happy to be a retired Spy Dog, especially now that I'm a mum, she thought, settling more comfortably in her chair.

Of course Lara would always be grateful to Professor Cortex for singling her out at his special animal spy school. The intensive training programme he put her on had completely changed her life.

After all, how many dogs can drive a car, defuse a bomb, understand several languages and have a black belt in karate? thought Lara. *And now I can pass all those skills on to the pups as well – and they're learning fast!*

And, even though she wasn't on active service, Lara's life was never dull.

In fact, sometimes it seems like adventures come looking for me, whether I like it or not! I've certainly had a few since I've been living here . . .

Lara yawned and tipped her sunhat over her eyes. The heat of the sun, the gentle movement of the deckchair and the sounds of family life drifting out from the Cooks' open back door mixed together with her memories of all her recent escapades. *I think I have the best of both worlds now . . .*

On the kitchen table Lara's smartphone suddenly buzzed into life. Lara had programmed it to play 'How Much is that Doggie in the Window?' if she had an email; 'Puppy Love' for a text message and Elvis Presley singing 'You Ain't Nothing but a Hound Dog' if she had a phone call. This time it was an email. It had just got to the bit about the waggly tail when Spud ran in from the garden.

Spud was a small, plump pup with jet-black fur like his dad. He picked up the smartphone carefully in his mouth and ran out to Lara.

'Wake up, Ma! You've got an email,' he woofed as he passed his mum the phone.

'I wasn't asleep!' protested Lara. 'I was just thinking . . . with my eyes closed.'

'In that case you were thinking and snoring at the same time!' chuckled Star. Star was a miniature version of her mum and just as intelligent. Spud and Star were a team. They were full of enthusiasm and always looking for adventure. They didn't mind the heat and they thought it was just a tiny bit boring that it seemed to make everyone else want to sit around doing not very much.

'Who's it from, Ma? What's it about?'

Lara touched the screen lazily with her paw. Then suddenly she sat bolt upright, wide awake.

'It's from the police,' she said. 'There's been a

break-in. Sophie's new teacher, Mr Thompson, was burgled this afternoon. The police want to know if we can help.'

'Wow!' said Spud. 'A real burglary in our village! That's never happened before, has it?'

'Well, not for a long, long time,' said Lara grimly. 'Not since I started our special animal neighbourhood watch team. Since then the local crime rate's been pretty close to zero.' She jumped out of her deckchair and marched quickly down the garden, the pups trotting along beside her.

'OK, pups, it's action stations! We need an emergency meeting of the whole team and we need it soon. Get the word out to everyone, straight away.'

'Right, Ma, what time and where?' barked Star efficiently.

'Seven o'clock on the village green,' said Lara. 'Surely someone must have seen something . . .'

3. Crimewatch

'So, what I need to know is, did anyone see anything unusual or suspicious at around three o'clock this afternoon?'

The neighbourhood watch team were lined up in front of Lara in order of size. The front row consisted of a hamster, two guinea pigs and George the tortoise, standing beside his special customized skateboard. Now that Professor Cortex had given George his own wheels he was never late for meetings any more.

In the second row was a mixture of cats and small dogs, including Spud and Star, all sitting

up smartly and paying attention. Under Lara's instruction the animals put their differences aside during meetings, but that didn't stop Sheba the Siamese swapping places quickly so she didn't have to sit next to Milo the lively Border terrier. Behind them were the bigger dogs: Labradors, retrievers, setters, an elderly Dalmatian and Danny Boy the greyhound. At the very back was the newest member of the team – a Shetland pony called Minstrel.

Lara's second-in-command, the pups' father, Potter – a handsome, shaggy, black pedigree – sat beside Lara at the front. All the animals were listening carefully to Lara's briefing.

'Mr Thompson only moved into that house a week ago and today someone broke in round the back and completely trashed it,' said Lara. 'But the really strange thing is that nothing was stolen.'

Felix put his paw up to show that he wanted to speak. 'Maybe the burglar was disturbed?' he suggested.

'Could be,' said Lara. 'Were any of you in the vicinity of the crime? Going for a walk with your owners, perhaps? Or –' she glanced at the cats – 'sitting on walls or climbing trees?'

The dogs and cats shook their heads. 'It was much too hot,' said Rex. 'I spent the afternoon indoors, lying beside my water bowl.'

'I was asleep in a flower bed,' volunteered Tiddles. 'Look, I've still got some petals in my fur!'

The other cats nodded. 'Far too hot to be out and about today.'

Lara looked at the animals in the front row. It wasn't much use asking the hamster – he slept all day at the best of times, and the guinea pigs lived on the wrong side of town.

'What about you, George?'

'It wasn't too hot for me,' said George. 'I just love this weather! But I didn't see anything, I'm afraid. I was busy practising my skate-boarding. I've got this great new move – shall I show you?'

Without waiting for an answer, George set off on his motorized skateboard and, after a while, very slowly lifted one front leg, held it in the air for a couple of seconds, then carefully put it back down again. After several suspense-filled seconds he then repeated the action in exactly the same way with his back leg. Then he turned the skateboard round and

brought it to a halt. The other animals clapped politely.

'It may not look much,' said George modestly, 'but that move represents a huge step for tortoise-kind. I'm going to call it – George's demon shell-tilt!'

'That's great, George,' said Lara, 'and I know it represents a lot of hard work and perseverance on your part, but we should really get back to business.'

'I think I may have seen something, Lara,' said a gentle voice. It was Minstrel the Shetland pony. 'I didn't think about it at the time, but I did see a car I didn't recognize going past my field into the village and then coming back again a little while later. I didn't see the driver, but I noticed the car because I was standing by the gate.'

Lara beckoned to Star and passed her a notebook. Star put a pen in her mouth and began to take notes. 'Do you have any idea what time this was?' asked Lara.

'Well, all I know is it was not long before my owner came home from school. That's why I was by the gate, you see. She always brings me an apple when she gets home.'

'OK, good information, Minstrel,' said Lara. She paused to check Star's notes.

'Your writing's nice and clear, Star, but "village" ends with a-g-e, not i-j. Never mind, we'll sort out the spelling later!'

Lara looked back at the pony; he was young and rather shy. Lara knew better than to hurry him. 'How about the car, Minstrel – can you tell me anything about that?'

'Oh dear, I don't really know much about cars, I'm afraid. It was blue, I think. Yes, definitely blue. It wasn't anything special, just an ordinary car. I can't tell you the registration number or anything – I'm not good at reading like you, Lara.'

'No, that's OK,' said Lara patiently. 'Just give

yourself a minute. Is there anything else at all you can remember?'

There was a long pause while Minstrel racked his brains. 'Oh, there is something,' he said at last. 'When the car was coming out of the village it was going really fast and it took the corner badly – it scraped against the wall on the passenger's side. That probably made quite a nasty scratch on the paintwork.'

'Brilliant!' said Lara. 'Well done! That's just the sort of information the police will want to have. Well, if no one else has anything to add, I think this meeting is over. I'll report back to the police immediately, and in the meantime everyone should be on Grade One alert – and I mean everyone! If you see or hear anything suspicious, act on it straight away; it doesn't matter if it turns out to be a false alarm. We don't want any more crime in our village.'

That's all very well, thought George to himself as he set off home on his skateboard, *but what we want and what we get are often two quite different things.*

4. At The Dirty Duck

Most of the customers at The Black Swan were drinking their beer outside that night. The pub, known to its regulars as The Dirty Duck, was in the middle of the city and there wasn't really a garden, but in the summer the landlady took down her washing line and put out empty barrels in the backyard so people could enjoy the evening air.

Only two men were sitting in the gloomy bar. They were tucked away in a corner by the dartboard, engrossed in conversation.

'Well, that was a total waste of time,' said the shorter of the two, a bulky man, almost as broad as he was tall, with a closely shaven head and thick, muscular arms. 'Are you sure H left it hidden in the house, Cliff?'

'Yes, Dale, I'm sure,' said the other man testily.

He was tall, slight, pale and nondescript – except for a nasty glint in his dark-grey eyes. 'He told me so himself, the day before he got caught.'

Even though they looked so different the two men were half-brothers. They had the same mother – a keen hill walker in her younger days who named her sons after geographical features – and they also shared the same dedication to a life of crime.

Cliff and Dale were two thirds of a successful gang of international art thieves. They had just managed to pull off a major robbery from the British Museum in London. The brothers didn't know anything about art or antiquities. They left that to their boss, Hugh Higsley-Hogbottom, known to the underworld as 'H'. H was educated, suave and super-cool. He knew exactly what to steal and who to sell it on to – but Dale and Cliff knew how to steal it.

'So H told you it was hidden in his house,' repeated Dale slowly. He paused to tip the contents of a small packet of peanuts into his mouth. 'Did he tell you where?'

Cliff gave his brother a withering look. 'Did he tell me where? Oooh, let me think. Yes, that's right, he said he'd put it on the shelf in the kitchen, and there's silly me letting us go and ransack the place when I knew exactly where it was all along.' He rolled his eyes. 'No, Dale, he did *not* tell me where he'd hidden it and now he's gone and got himself locked up – for not paying his taxes, of all things – and that teacher's moved into his house instead.'

'Well, we know it's not there now, anyway, don't we?' said Dale sulkily. 'We turned the place over good and proper. So I suppose we might as well give up.'

Cliff snorted and spluttered beer all over the table. 'Give up! Are you mad? We risked a lot breaking into that stupid museum. Robbery with violence, Dale. It doesn't go down too well in court, in case you hadn't noticed. And it didn't help that you went and fired your shooter, either.'

Dale's hand automatically checked the inside pocket of his jacket. 'No, the Old Bill aren't too keen on shooters,' he agreed. He knew this from bitter experience, and yet somehow his time in prison still hadn't made him change his ways.

'If the cops catch us, we'll be banged up for a long, long time,' went on Cliff, 'and we haven't even got anything to show for it!'

A young couple came into the bar and looked like they might sit down nearby. Dale gave them his very worst scowl and they hurriedly moved outside.

Cliff lowered his voice. 'H had a collector in Geneva lined up ready and waiting to buy it. He was going to pay tens of millions of euros – in cash!' He put his face up close to Dale's and looked into his eyes. 'We *deserve* that money, Dale. The guy in Geneva's waiting. If

20

we can give him what he wants, he'll pass that dosh over to us. We can keep it all and get out of the country before H gets out of the slammer. No one will ever find us.'

Dale nodded slowly. 'Makes sense, bruv. I've always fancied a nice little place in the sun. So you say we keep on looking?'

'That's right,' nodded Cliff.

Dale tipped half a packet of pickled-onion-flavoured crisps into his mouth and thought hard. You could tell from his face that he usually let someone else do the thinking. Then he had an idea.

'Maybe the teacher found it when he moved in?'

'Just what I was thinking,' agreed Cliff. 'He'd probably know a bit about all that old museum stuff, wouldn't he, being a teacher? He might guess it was worth a bit. Maybe he's going to try to flog it himself.'

Dale smiled a nasty smile. 'We can't have that, can we, bruv?'

'No, we can't,' said Cliff. 'You know what? I think we might have to take another little trip to the country . . .'

5. The School Run

Who's that? Lara's sharp ears heard footsteps on the stairs. Ben was tiptoeing down as quietly as he could – he even remembered to miss out the stair that always creaked – but when he opened the kitchen door, Lara was out of her basket and standing ready to greet him.

'Sorry, Lara, I know it's the middle of the night,' said Ben, giving her a pat. 'It's so hot I just had to get a glass of water.'

Ben was the eldest of the Cook children and he and Lara had a special bond. It was on Ben's tenth birthday that the family had found Lara at the RSPCA animal shelter and Ben had always felt that Lara was really his dog. Lara felt the same. She loved spending time with Ben, playing football, swimming or fishing in the river.

Ben crept past Spud and Star, both fast asleep in their baskets, and took a glass out of the cupboard. He was just about to turn on the tap when he suddenly froze. At exactly the same moment Lara's sticky-up ear began to twitch and she looked quickly towards the back door. They had both heard a noise outside.

'What is it, girl?' whispered Ben.

I don't know. Something's out there – or somebody. Sounded like someone climbing over the fence. Could be a fox or could be – Lara rushed to the door and gave a low, threatening growl. *Whoever you are, don't you DARE come near my family!*

She was just about to move on to some really fierce barks when she heard a doggie whisper from outside. 'Psst, Lara, it's me, Potter!'

'Potter!' Lara's tail started to wag. 'What are you doing? I thought you were a burglar!'

'Urgent message, Lara. I've brought it to you myself. One of the cats has seen something – a blue car with a scratch on the passenger's side; it's parked outside the school.'

Lara immediately snapped into her official Spy Dog mode. 'How long ago was this?' she asked.

'Just a couple of minutes. Sheba miaowed the message to Scottie; he barked it on to me and I came straight round.'

'OK, Potter, thanks. I'll take it from here.'

Lara looked around for her phone. Meanwhile the pups had woken up and heard the conversation. They couldn't contain their excitement.

'It's Mr Thompson's burglar. He's back again!' woofed Spud.

'We've got to catch him this time!' barked Star.

Ben could tell something was going on, but of course he didn't know what. 'What's happening, Lara?' he asked.

Ben, you can help me here! Lara grabbed a pencil in her mouth and scrawled a hurried message on the bottom of Mrs Cook's shopping list:

POLICE → SCHOOL

BURGLAR!

Then she tapped the emergency number for the police on to her phone and passed it to Ben.

'Oh, I get it,' said Ben. 'That must have been a message from the neighbourhood watch.'

Ben gave the information to the emergency operator quickly and calmly while Lara expertly slid back the bolt on the back door.

'Are we going to the school, Ma?' woofed Star.

'I am – and every second counts! If I hurry I can get there before the police – but you two pups must stay here and guard the house.'

The pups were disappointed, but they didn't argue. *After all, if there are baddies about, someone's got to take care of the family.*

'I'll come with you, Lara,' said Ben. 'Can I just go and get dressed?'

Lara shook her head emphatically. *No time!* She rushed outside to find her bike. Lara was an excellent cyclist and often went for long rides with the children. Ben followed, pushing his bare feet into his trainers.

'Don't go without me!' It was Sophie, Ben's sister, two years younger, but very brave. She had heard the barking and Ben's voice downstairs and had come to investigate.

I haven't got time to argue, thought Lara, as she pressed her back feet hard down on the pedals and began to cycle as if her life depended on it.

They made an unusual sight, three speeding

cyclists on the empty night road – one in *Star Wars* pyjamas, one in a *Hello Kitty* nightdress and one a black and white dog with a very determined expression.

Lara took the lead. Halfway along the road they caught up with Potter who was making for the school as well. 'We'll take the short cut,' said Lara as she hurtled down a side lane towards the railway level crossing.

'I'm coming too!' Little Scottie came bounding over a garden wall, his short, black legs moving faster than they'd ever done before.

Just at that moment the lights beside the crossing began to flash and the barricades came creaking slowly down.

Oh no! There's a train coming! Lara squeezed her brakes and brought the bike to an emergency stop. She was going so fast that she nearly went head first over the handlebars. Behind her, Ben and Sophie pulled up too and Potter took the opportunity to catch his breath – but Scottie kept on going!

'Stop, Scottie!' barked Lara.

'What's the problem?' replied Scottie. 'We can get round these funny fence things easily if we're quick. Come on!'

'No, Scottie!' shouted Ben.

In a flash Lara realized that Scottie didn't know about level crossings. He was quite a young dog and not one of the brightest members of her team. Of course he couldn't read the warning signs. He had no idea of the deathly danger he was just about to face.

'STOP!' she bellowed, and with one flying leap, hurled herself towards the little dog, catching her teeth in his tartan collar just as he was about to dodge behind the barricade. Using all her strength she flung him away from danger. Then she stood over him with one paw firmly on his chest so that he couldn't move.

'You must never, EVER cross a level crossing once the lights are flashing, Scottie,' said Lara. 'It means there's a train coming and –' Her voice was drowned by the roar of a night train speeding down the line. As the heavy carriages hurtled past, Scottie saw and understood.

'OK,' said Lara, getting on her bike. 'We should be able to get across now.' But no, the lights kept flashing and the barricades stayed down. Another train was on its way. This was an engine going back to the local depot. It was travelling at a much more sedate pace. Lara tapped her handlebars impatiently; Potter started running on the spot. The driver saw the children and slowed right down.

'What are you two doing out at this time of night?' he called from his window. He hadn't noticed Lara in the shadow of a tree.

'Er, just keeping fit!' said Ben. It would take too long to explain.

'You can take this keep-fit malarkey too far, if you ask me,' said the driver. 'Oh well, good luck to you!'

As the engine chugged on through, the driver turned to give the children a wave and caught a glimpse of Lara.

I've really got to stop doing these late shifts, he thought, giving his head a shake. *I could have sworn I saw a dog on a bike back there.*

At last the barriers went up and the path was clear. The cyclists raced off down the lane with Potter and a rather quiet Scottie following behind.

As they reached the school gates, Lara saw immediately that the lock had been neatly picked. The school's front door was swinging open too, but there was no sign of a car.

Sheba the Siamese cat appeared out of the

bushes. 'You're too late,' she miaowed. 'They've gone.'

'Did you get a look at them?' asked Lara.

'Not really – only from the back. There were two of them, both men. One was tall and slim and one was short and stocky.'

Seconds later a police car arrived – and so did Mr Thompson. Mr Thompson had obviously got dressed in a hurry. He was wearing his T-shirt back to front and inside out so the label was sticking out at the front and his hair was standing on end in a very unusual style. He greeted the children and Lara cheerfully. 'Hi,

Sophie! Hello, Ben – and Lara too! The police told me you raised the alarm. I don't know – two break-ins in two days. What *is* going on around here?'

'It seems the thieves have left the property,' said PC Brown. 'Could you come in and tell us what's missing, sir?'

Everyone went into the school. It was hard to believe that anything out of the ordinary had happened there that night. Every classroom looked just as usual; the cloakrooms too. There was an odd sock lying on a bench in the hall, but it seemed like the cleaners could have found that behind a radiator. The head teacher's desk was a bit untidy, but Mr Thompson said it often looked like that. Then Mr Thompson opened the staffroom door.

'Wow, what a mess!' he said, gazing at the overturned chairs and scattered papers. The noticeboard was ripped off the wall and all the teachers' coffee mugs had been swept out of the cupboard on to the floor. With every step he took across the room, Mr Thompson crunched spilt sugar and instant coffee into the carpet. Yet, even though he looked very hard, he couldn't find anything missing.

'Just vandals,' said PC Brown as they secured the gates with a new padlock. 'Most probably teenagers from the town with nothing better to do than go round making trouble. Well, thank you everyone, you can all go back to your beds.'

There's more to this than meets the eye, thought Lara as they cycled home with the first rays of sunlight appearing in the sky. *Those two men deactivated an alarm system and broke through two secure locks. I'd bet my last custard cream that they are professional thieves. I'd say they're looking for something. But what? And, just as importantly, why?*

6. The Experiment

The next day was Saturday. Spud and Star were practising keepy-uppies in the garden when they heard the doorbell. 'Race you!' shouted Spud and the two pups hurtled through the house, jostling each other as they both tried to get to the front door first.

Ollie beat them both as he happened to be coming down the stairs at the time. Six-year-old Ollie was the youngest of the three Cook children. He had to stand on tiptoe to reach the latch. Spud and Star both jumped up too, but they were much too small and only succeeded in getting in Ollie's way.

At last the door was open and Ollie and the pups looked out at the strange sight in front of them. It was a tall, rather wobbly pile of books with a pair of pale, hairy legs poking out from

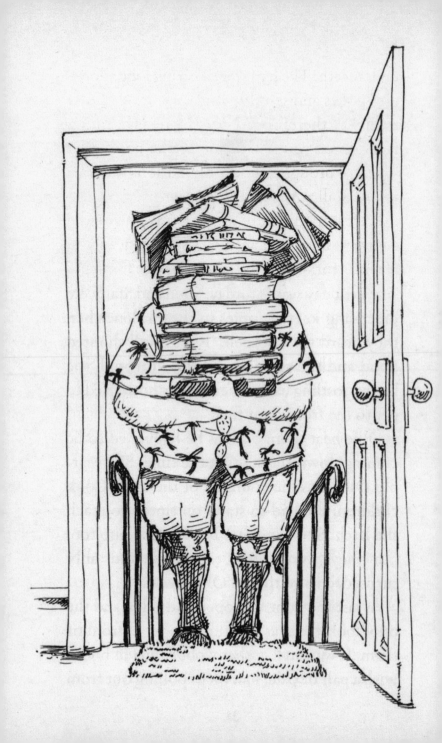

underneath. The legs were wearing long shorts, grey socks and sensible sandals.

'Hello, there!' Professor Cortex's beaming face peered round the side of the book pile. 'I've just brought some contributions for your mum's stall at the school fete.'

Professor Maximus Cortex was one of the country's most brilliant scientists and inventors. He had worked for the Secret Service for many years and was responsible for training all the highly skilled undercover spy animals. Lara had been his very first graduate and was still his star pupil, but he had high hopes that Spud and Star might soon be following in her footsteps.

'I know the fete's not till next weekend,' he said, 'but I'm off on holiday today.'

That explains the outfit! Star smiled to herself. She had never seen the professor in that Hawaiian shirt before – it was green and orange and covered in palm trees!

Soon the professor was sitting comfortably in the kitchen surrounded by all three children and all three dogs while Mrs Cook put his books in a cardboard box ready to take to school. Lara made him a cup of coffee and Sophie offered him a chocolate digestive. Spud looked longingly at the biscuit tin, but Lara shook her head. *Really, Spud, you've only just had your breakfast!*

'I was also wondering whether Lara and the pups might like to take part in a little experiment for a friend of mine,' said the professor. 'If that's OK with you, of course?' he added, looking at Mrs Cook.

Oooh yay! woofed Spud. *What is it, Prof? Secret spy stuff? Testing stun guns and ejector seats and cars that can fly?*

'It's an experiment to see whether children's performance at school improves if there are animals around,' went on the professor.

Not spy stuff, then, thought Spud, a bit disappointed.

'My friend is looking into the idea that having a pet in the classroom may actually help children learn. It's just for the next couple of weeks until the end of term.' He looked at Lara and the pups. 'All you'd have to do is go to the local school every day and sit in on the lessons. You don't actually have to *do* the lessons — unless you want to, of course; just be around the children.'

'At my school?' asked Ollie excitedly. 'Mine

and Sophie's?' Now Ben was twelve, he went to secondary school in the nearby town.

'That's right,' said the professor. 'Spud would be in your class, Ollie. Star would be in Mrs Lawson's class and Lara would be in Mr Thompson's class with Sophie.'

Lara gave the professor a questioning look.

'It sounds like an interesting experiment,' said Mrs Cook. 'I'd be happy to let them take part.'

Ollie jumped up and down. 'It'll be SO cool!' he said. 'We can play together at lunchtime and I can show my friends all the brilliant things the pups can do.'

'I'm not sure it will improve *Ollie's* performance, having Spud in his class,' said Mum doubtfully as Ollie and Spud did a celebratory dance like two footballers who had just scored a goal. 'But you never know, I suppose.'

Ollie collapsed breathlessly beside their guest again. 'Have you invented any new gadgets recently?' he asked.

Professor Cortex chuckled. 'I thought you might ask me that, young man,' he said. 'Do you still have a sandpit in your garden? Or are you too grown up for that sort of thing nowadays?'

'No, we've still got one,' said Ollie, looking interested. 'Why?'

'Well, if you go out there, I'll just get my bag,' said the scientist. 'Then I'll show you something you might find interesting.'

Everyone went into the garden except the professor and Lara. The professor hurried to his car, which was parked on the road outside, and Lara followed him.

When they were alone Lara looked the professor squarely in the eye. *Come on, Prof, spill the beans. There's more to this 'school experiment' than meets the eye, isn't there? Why do you want me in Mr Thompson's class exactly?*

'All right, GM451, I know you're on to me!' laughed her old friend. 'The experiment is completely genuine, but, yes, I do also have an ulterior motive for sending you and the pups into the school.'

Lara nodded. *Keep talking.*

'The truth is that I'm not at all happy about what's been going on around here – those two mysterious break-ins where nothing was taken. I don't understand it, but it seems to have something to do with Mr Thompson. I'd just like you and the pups to keep your eyes open while I'm away. It might be nothing but . . .'

Yep, Prof, I couldn't agree more. It might be nothing, but it might be something too. I think it's a great idea for us to be in the school. We can keep an eye on Mr Thompson and on Sophie and Ollie too.

Lara gave the professor a big nod and closed one eye in a wink.

'I knew you'd understand,' he said with a smile.

7. Great Gadgets

The children always loved seeing the professor's latest inventions. Some of his gadgets went straight off to be used exclusively by MI5 and MI6, but others were designed to be sold to the general public to raise money for future research.

Everyone gathered round the sandpit, watching as he produced a bizarre-looking contraption, including two buckets of different sizes, a plastic spade, lots of cogs and wheels, and a small, solar-powered engine.

'As I'm going on holiday to the seaside I thought I'd design –' the professor paused for dramatic effect and then said with a flourish – 'an automatic sandcastle-builder! Ta-da! Just watch this!'

He put the contraption in the sandpit, stood

well back and zapped it with a remote control. There was a faint buzzing sound and the spade began to dig, filling one of the buckets with sand.

'This is the basic program,' explained the professor as the machine turned the bucket over and lifted it up to reveal a perfect little sandcastle. 'But now watch this!'

He zapped with a different button. This time the machine moved round the sandpit, making a circle of small sandcastles and finally adding a bigger one in the middle, using a different bucket.

'I'm working on several more programs to produce various designs,' said the professor. 'Moats, turrets, all that sort of thing . . . But I'm taking this prototype to the beach to try it out. The great thing is I'll be able to make sandcastles while I'm sitting in my deckchair reading a scientific journal! Isn't that fantastic? What do you think, kids?'

There was a second's silence.

'It's really good,' said Sophie kindly.

'But?' said the professor. 'It's OK, young lady, I can hear there's a "but". Don't worry, I can take it!'

'But maybe the really fun thing about sandcastles is actually building them *yourself*?' suggested Sophie hesitantly.

The professor scratched his head. 'Hmm, I see what you mean,' he said at last. 'Well, never mind, I'll treat it as a work in progress. I'm sure I can adapt the idea somehow. Now, let me see, what else have I got . . . ah yes!'

He took his hands out of his bag and held them in front of him with his fists loosely closed. 'What do you think of *this*?'

'What?' chorused the children.

'Oh, can't you see it?' teased the professor. 'Ben, would you do a simple karate chop movement through the air between my hands? Not too hard, just a quick slice towards the ground.'

'OK,' said Ben, mystified. 'Here goes . . . Yow!' Ben's hand stopped in mid-air directly in line with the professor's fists. 'There's something in the way!'

'That's right and that something is . . . invisible string!' said the professor proudly. 'I've discovered that if I coat some strong thread with a special light-reflective mixture, it becomes invisible to the naked eye. Feel it, everyone! It's really there, but you just can't see it!'

'Wow!' said Sophie. Even Mrs Cook was impressed.

'Could you coat *me* in your special mixture?' asked Ollie. 'Then I could be invisible too?'

'I'm afraid it wouldn't work on you, Ollie,' said the professor. 'It has to be something that's really very fine, like thread or wire. You can have a sample, though. In fact you can all have one – I've got plenty. I've already run this idea past MI5 and I can tell you they're *very* interested!'

The children each took what looked like a plain bit of cardboard, but when they touched it they could feel the invisible string wrapped round.

'I can't wait to show this to my friends!' said Ollie, 'Oh, hey – we can show them together, Spud!' he added, remembering that Lara and the pups would be going to school with him too.

The professor looked at his watch. 'Goodness me, I should be going. I haven't even started my packing yet! I've just got one other new invention here; I'll show you quickly.'

He produced a rather scruffy-looking brown paper bag and took out a small, black capsule. 'I call this my black-out capsule,' he said. 'It can make any room entirely private in seconds.'

Very useful for spies, thought Lara.

'How does it work?' asked Sophie, looking at the capsule doubtfully.

'Allow me to demonstrate,' said the professor, leading the way back into the kitchen.

'Now, you have some delightful curtains at your window, Mrs Cook, so if you wanted privacy you could simply pull them closed. But let's suppose you didn't have any curtains; perhaps you were in an office or a train . . .' He suddenly hurled the capsule at the kitchen window. It broke open and a pool of what looked like thick, black ink began to spread across the glass.

Mrs Cook gasped. Lara blinked. *I think you've gone too far this time, Professor!*

The black substance covered the window perfectly, stopping neatly at the edges. The sunny room was instantly dark and Ben had to turn on the light.

'It would be good for people who need to sleep in the daytime too,' said the professor thoughtfully. 'I hadn't thought of that before.'

'It's brilliant,' said Mrs Cook, 'but, er, how do you get it off?'

'Oh, no problem at all,' laughed the professor. 'I call it intelligent plastic. Look – it just peels straight off if you pull it!' Sure enough, the professor lifted up a corner of the coating and the whole thing came away, leaving the window looking as good as new.

'Impressive!' said Ben. 'Professor, you're a genius!'

'Oh no, not at all,' said the scientist modestly, shaking his head. 'I just do what I can, you know. You children can have a sample one of these too, if you like, and now I really must be off!'

After the professor had gone Mrs Cook picked up one of the books he had given her for the stall. It was called *Investigations in Molecules and Matter.* She blew the dust off the cover and glanced inside. As far as Mrs Cook was concerned, it might as well have been written in a foreign language – she couldn't understand a word! 'Oh well,' she sighed. 'These might not be the *first* books we sell at the fete, but I suppose someone may buy them eventually!'

Spud and Star were so excited about going to school that they wanted to pack their school bags straight away. Ollie found them pencil cases, and helped sharpen some pencils and crayons for them.

Lara looked on thoughtfully. *Like it or not, I get the feeling that another Spy Dog mission is under way.*

8. The Monster Machine

'Welcome to Year Five, Lara!' said Mr Thompson. 'As you know the experiment simply requires you to be in the room, so feel free to join in with our lessons as little or as much as you like.'

Everyone in the village knew about Lara and her special skills, although they made a point of never discussing it with strangers. Mr Thompson was well aware that most of his lessons would be far too easy for Lara.

'If you just want to sit in the corner and observe, that's fine too,' he added.

Oh no! Lara shook her head vigorously. *That's way too boring for me!*

'I'm sure Lara would like to get involved,' said Sophie. 'She always helps us with our homework and she's taught the pups loads of things too.'

49

Lara nodded enthusiastically.

'Well, that's great!' said Mr Thompson, looking pleased. 'This is a lively class and I could certainly use a helper, if you're willing!'

Lara liked Mr Thompson. He was young and funny and he clearly loved his job. She was secretly rather proud to be his new classroom assistant.

As the children began their number work, Lara strolled between their tables, gently pointing out any mistakes with her paw. Sometimes she put a pencil in her mouth and made a small correction – she was particularly strong on maths.

Later in the morning, when Sophie's friend Grant was making a list of creatures that live in Antarctica and got stuck after 'seal' and 'polar bear', Lara did such a funny impersonation of a waddling penguin that poor Grant almost fell off his chair laughing.

Lara could easily work the interactive whiteboard and she happily trotted around the classroom giving out worksheets and collecting books, carrying them carefully in her mouth. Then, when Molly Jenkins suddenly got a nosebleed, it was Lara who found her some

tissues and went with her to sit quietly in the office for a while.

'I don't know how I ever managed without you,' said Mr Thompson at lunchtime. 'You and I make a great team, Lara!'

That's right! thought Lara happily. *We're a lean, mean teaching machine! I like this job almost as much as my old one!*

After lunch Mr Thompson started telling the class about the ancient Greeks. Lara was fascinated. She hadn't studied much ancient history with the professor and she always liked learning anything new. She listened, wide-eyed, as Mr Thompson explained about the clever people who lived in Athens over two thousand years ago.

It was another hot day and, as she glanced through the window at the school field, Lara noticed that Ollie's teacher had taken her class outside. The children were sitting cross-legged underneath a big, shady tree while their teacher sat on a chair reading to them.

There's Ollie – and Spud, sitting beside him. Both of them being as good as gold, thought Lara proudly. *Spud isn't fidgeting at all. He must be really interested!*

In the distance Lara could hear the sound of the school gardener mowing the grass with his big ride-on lawnmower. The fresh, grassy smell wafted into the classroom.

This is lovely, thought Lara. *A perfect afternoon.*

She noticed the noise of the mower was growing a little louder. *He must be coming this way.* Then Lara glanced towards the sound –

the lawnmower, a powerful red machine like
a miniature tractor, was certainly coming their
way. It seemed to be gaining speed as well, but
instantly Lara realized that there was no one
driving it! *That mower is out of control – and it's
heading straight for the children!*

'So, does anyone know where the first
Olympic Games were held?' asked Mr
Thompson, looking round the room. 'Lara!
Where are you going?'

For no obvious reason, Lara had jumped up
and leapt out of the open classroom window.

A second later she was racing off across the grass, barking wildly.

Spud! Spud! Look out! Get everyone out of the way! she woofed.

Spud heard his mum and looked round. He saw the lawnmower charging towards them and started barking too and pulling at the sleeve of Ollie's T-shirt.

Ollie, look behind you! There's a monster machine on the loose!

'Shhh, Spud, behave yourself,' said Ollie. 'Listen to the story.'

Ollie's teacher looked up from her book, but from where she was sitting she couldn't see anything wrong. She just assumed the gardener was cutting the grass nearby.

'If you don't stop barking, Spud, you'll have to go back in the classroom,' she said sternly.

Meanwhile Mr Thompson had seen what was happening and he too had leapt out of the window and was running, shouting and waving his arms.

And the runaway lawnmower was gaining speed.

Lara ran her very fastest. Her heart was banging in her chest and she was gasping for breath. *If I don't do something, those children will be mown down like daisies.*

As the machine closed in on them, Ollie's teacher suddenly realized what all the fuss was about. She jumped to her feet and screamed. The children all started screaming too. No one knew which way to run.

But Lara was there. With the runaway mower only seconds away from the first child, Lara leapt into the driver's seat and wrenched at the steering wheel. The machine veered sideways, crashing into the tree, hitting its trunk with enormous force. Then it tipped over, hurling Lara out as it rolled. The mower lay on its side with its engine throbbing and its blades still spinning, but Lara lay in a crumpled heap, completely still.

'Come on, Lara, wake up, old girl!' The Spy Dog felt something wet trickling down her face. *Is that blood?*

Lara could feel a dull pain at the back of her head where she must have hit the ground. She opened one eye and saw Mr Thompson's worried face looking down at her. She opened the other eye and realized he was gently sponging her forehead with warm water.

'It's OK, you've had a nasty bump and you just passed out for a couple of minutes.'

Lara moved her legs experimentally. *Seems like I'm still in one piece.*

'You did a fantastic job, Lara. I've never seen anyone move so fast,' said Mr Thompson. 'Thank goodness you were here this afternoon. If it hadn't been for you, there could have been a very nasty accident.'

Lara was fully conscious now. *I'm sorry, Mr Thompson, but you've got it wrong. Lawnmowers don't do things like that by themselves. Someone had tampered with that machine and jammed the throttle on. Someone had aimed it at those children – someone who didn't care what happened next. Whatever happened this afternoon I know one thing for sure – it was no accident.*

9. Painting Plates

'Nice one, bruv, so did you see what happened?' Cliff was talking to Dale on his mobile phone as he made for his usual corner in The Dirty Duck.

'Nah, the school gardener came back and I had to leg it – but I heard lots of kids screaming and dogs barking and then a really big crash. I'm guessing someone definitely got hurt,' said Dale with a horrible smile. He was holding his phone in one hand and steering very badly with the other as he sped along the lane away from the village.

'Well, that should put the frighteners on our friend the teacher,' said Cliff. 'He'll know that, next time, it just might be him!'

'That's the idea,' laughed Dale. 'So when we pay him our next little visit I think he'll be more than happy to help us, don't you?'

'I think he will, Dale, I think he will. Now he knows the kind of people he's up against, I think he might just spill the entire can of beans and tell us everything we need to know.'

'Costa del Sunshine, here we come!' yelled Dale, accelerating away after his car grazed the wheel of a woman on her bicycle and sent her flying into the hedge.

But Dale and Cliff were completely wrong. Mr Thompson knew nothing of the ways of the criminal underworld and he had no idea

that the incident with the lawnmower was meant as a threat. Once he was sure that Lara wasn't badly hurt, he thought no more about it and came whistling into school each day, just as cheerful and relaxed as ever.

Lara, however, remained on full alert and she warned the pups to be the same. 'I know you're having lots of fun at school,' she said. 'But remember, Spy Dogs never drop their guard. If you notice anything odd, come straight to me.'

Spud and Star nodded solemnly.

'Everything seems normal,' went on Lara, 'but there's definitely something strange going on around here — and one way or another I intend to get to the bottom of it.'

As the pets-in-the-classroom experiment continued, it became increasingly clear that having Lara and the pups in the school was good news. The teachers reported excellent results and were pleased with the way their classes were working.

'I thought the animals might be a distraction,' said the head, 'but funnily enough they seem to be helping the children to concentrate. It makes me wonder whether every class should have a resident dog!'

On Friday, Year Five were continuing their studies of the ancient Greeks by making decorated plates.

'We prepared the plates last week,' Mr Thompson explained to Lara. 'Now we're going to paint them in the style of ancient Greek pottery.'

I know someone who'll enjoy that! thought Lara. Sophie was very artistic and loved anything that involved painting or drawing.

'But first I want everyone to research images on the Internet,' Mr Thompson went on, addressing the class. 'Find as many examples of ancient Greek pottery as you can and choose a design that you'd like to copy. The finished results should look as authentic as possible. You can do one too, Lara, if you like. I've got a spare plate you can have.'

Lara wagged her tail. *I'm not great at painting, but I'll give it a go!*

Lara and Sophie sat side by side at the class computers, searching on various websites. Sophie soon found an image that appealed to her.

'Look at this, Lara,' she said, pointing to a picture of a horse with huge wings. 'It's called Pegasus, the flying horse. I'm going to print it out and see if I can copy it.

The design was really striking, but Lara was more interested in the text that went with the picture. It was an article from a news website. The headline was:

PRICELESS GREEK PLATE STOLEN
FROM LONDON MUSEUM

It went on to say that, only a few weeks earlier, thieves had broken into the British Museum and stolen an important and very valuable piece of ancient Greek pottery.

What a shame, thought Lara. *A precious bit of the past like that should be somewhere where everyone can see it. Looks like that museum might need better security!*

'Found anything yet, Lara?' asked Mr Thompson.

Lara shook her head. *I need something that's easier to copy*, she thought and began clicking and scrolling with increasing desperation. *Those ancient Greek guys were good! A bit too good for a doggie painter like me.*

In the end Lara found a picture of a dish with three big painted fish following each other around inside it. She decided to go for that.

Looking at those fish is making me hungry! thought Lara. *Or maybe it's the smell of shepherd's pie coming from the school canteen. Oh good, there's the bell for lunch!*

By the end of the afternoon, Year Five had finished painting their plates. Lara thought Sophie's was very impressive — the black outline of the flying horse against the red background of the plate looked almost as good as the one they'd seen on the Internet. She wasn't so pleased with her own efforts. *I definitely need more practice. My fish look more like three bananas!*

Lara and Sophie met the others in the playground at hometime.

'My class went swimming today, Ma!' said Star. 'It was brilliant. I taught two non-swimmers to swim – doggie-paddle, of course!'

I wonder what their parents will say when they hear their children were taught to swim by a puppy? thought Lara, smiling to herself.

Gran was waiting by the gates and they all walked home together. They had just got to the front door when Ollie suddenly stopped and hit his forehead with his hand. 'Duh! I've forgotten my school bag!' he said.

'Oh, Ollie, not *again*!' groaned Sophie. Ollie could be very forgetful.

Spud put his paw in the air in the way he'd learnt to do at school, to ask if he could speak. 'Shall Star and I go back and get it?' he asked. 'I bet I know exactly where it is.'

'OK, then,' said Lara. 'But come straight

back, be careful crossing the roads – and don't get into any mischief!'

Meanwhile Mr Thompson had decided to stay and sort out the art cupboard. The next day was the school fete and he wanted the classroom to be super-tidy in case any parents looked in. He took everything out of the cupboard and began to pile it on the tables so he could get in and clean the shelves.

All the children had gone home and all the teachers had followed, but Mr Thompson carried on happily organizing piles of different-coloured paper and card and finding new homes for scissors and crayons. Soon he was the only one left in the school.

Apart, that is, from two men in white painters' overalls who, at that moment, were strolling in through the front door. One was tall and one was short and they both had a nasty look in their eyes.

10. Pups to the Rescue!

Mr Thompson was just about to put a big roll of sugar paper back into the cupboard when he heard someone breathing heavily behind him. Before he had time to turn, a thick arm wrapped round his throat and held him in a tight headlock. Whoever it was didn't seem very friendly.

Then a voice growled in his ear. 'Now, we don't want any trouble, do we? So let's do this nice and quietly, no shouting for help or anything like that, eh?'

'N-n-no, OK,' agreed Mr Thompson.

The headlock loosened and Mr Thompson was suddenly bundled into the cupboard. The door slammed shut, the key turned and he found himself trapped inside in the dark.

'Nice one, bruv,' muttered Cliff. 'Now he'll never know what we look like!'

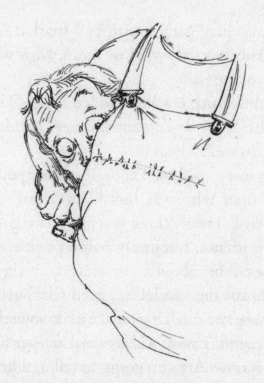

'I'm not just a pretty face, you know,' Dale replied, contorting his features in a smile that could *never* be described as pretty.

'OK, teacher, listen up,' said Cliff, raising his voice. 'You know what we want – and *we* know you've got it.'

Mr Thompson was mystified. 'I haven't got anything!' he protested. 'Well, there's some poster paint in here and some paper and . . . glue and . . . I suppose some quite nice crayons.'

'Don't play games with us!' snarled Cliff. 'You know exactly what we mean. Now where have you put it?'

'Think hard, teacher,' added Dale. 'Think very hard. We don't want another "accident", now, do we?'

'I'm sorry,' said Mr Thompson, quite politely for a man who was locked in a hot, dark cupboard. 'I really think you must have got the wrong person. I honestly haven't a clue what you're talking about.'

'Oh, cut the cackle!' snapped Cliff, getting really angry now. 'Don't make us do something we'd regret. I want a one-word answer and I want it now. Are you going to tell us where it is, YES or NO?'

Mr Thompson was baffled. 'Well . . . no,' he replied, 'because –'

'That, teacher,' interrupted Cliff in a voice like ice, 'is the *wrong* answer.'

Cliff looked at his brother and nodded slowly. Dale reached inside his jacket pocket . . .

Meanwhile, Spud and Star had raced each other back to school and found Ollie's school bag still hanging on his peg in the cloakroom.

'He'd forget his own feet if they weren't on the end of his legs,' laughed Star.

The pups were just leaving the building when they noticed two men in painters' overalls going into Mr Thompson's classroom.

'That's funny!' said Star. 'There isn't any decorating being done in the school at the moment, is there?'

'No,' said Spud thoughtfully. He glanced at the road outside. 'Look! It's a blue car.'

'And those two men –' said Star.

'. . . are the burglars, I bet!' added Spud. 'Yikes! Mum was right. There is something going on around here. Come on, sis, now's our chance to catch some baddies!'

The two pups raced down the corridor to the classroom. They arrived in time to see Mr Thompson being pushed into the cupboard by the two unpleasant-looking men.

'Be careful, Spud,' whispered Star. 'We've got to play it cool. If we rush in now, we could end up in the cupboard too.'

The pups flattened themselves against the wall outside the door and listened as Cliff and Dale questioned Mr Thompson. They could see things were looking nasty.

'What shall we do?' whispered Star. 'We're too small to overpower them.'

They looked at each other in desperation. Then Spud had an idea.

'The invisible string!' he said. 'There's some in Ollie's school bag!' He rummaged in the bag and pulled it out. 'Spy Pups to the rescue!' he woofed.

The two pups ran up to the men, wagging their tails and trying to look cute, pretending to be normal puppies. Of course the villains couldn't see that the pups were holding invisible string in their mouths. They weren't exactly friendly all the same.

'Get out of here, mutt,' said Cliff, aiming a kick at Star's head. 'What are dogs doing in a school anyway?'

Star dodged neatly out of the way and ran round Cliff's legs, still innocently wagging her tail. Spud moved in the opposite direction past Dale. Suddenly the two men felt something against their ankles.

'Round and round, Spud! Round and round!' woofed Star. The pups circled the men, wrapping the string round their legs and tying them together.

'Aargh! What's happening?' Cliff tried to move, but pulled his brother along too. It was like a bizarre three-legged race. They both staggered and struggled to stand up straight.

'Keep going!' barked Star. 'We're doing well!'

'Something's got us,' gasped Dale. 'It's stopping us from moving!'

'But there's nothing there!' said Cliff. 'Those dogs aren't even touching us! I don't like this at all!'

The pups kept up their circling movements, crossing each other as they passed, until they finally ran out of string. By this time the villains were both terrified out of their wits. Hobbling and tripping their way from the classroom, they scrabbled at their legs in an attempt to escape from whatever it was that was forcing them together.

The pups watched gleefully as, once they'd got outside, Dale made a sudden dash for the car, but pulled Cliff after him. Cliff toppled into Dale and both of them fell on the ground. Then neither of them could stand up. In the end Dale had to crawl along the gravel path with Cliff riding piggyback. Eventually the two villains managed to unravel themselves enough to get in their car. They drove away, their faces white with fear and their hands shaking.

Star made a note of the car registration number while Spud pushed a chair up to the cupboard door and, holding the key carefully in his mouth, managed to turn the lock. The door swung open and Mr Thompson staggered out, blinking and rubbing his eyes.

'Wow! Thanks, pups!' he said, giving them both a grateful pat. 'I was beginning to wonder when those men were going to let me out.'

Spud looked sideways at Star. 'He doesn't

realize, does he? If it hadn't been for us – and the professor's string – he might *never* have got out of there . . . alive.'

11. A Letter from 'Daddy'

'You were both absolutely brilliant,' said Lara to the pups next day as they put the finishing touches to a batch of fairy cakes for the school fete. 'The professor will be very proud of you. You followed Spy Dog procedure perfectly: assessing the situation, taking minimal risks and rescuing the hostage without any violence. Well done!'

'Thanks, Ma!' The pups glanced at each other and smiled. They both felt ten feet tall.

'You were quite right to take the car's registration number, Star,' went on Lara, 'and the excellent descriptions you both gave mean the police now have two clear suspects – both known criminals. They're looking for them now.'

'So, can we have a cherry as a reward?' asked Spud. The pups were decorating the tops of the cakes with glacé cherries.

'You can have a whole cake if you like,' smiled Lara. 'In fact I think I'll have one too – just to make sure they're all right . . .'

'I still don't understand it, though,' added Lara after she'd finished her cake. 'What do people like that want with Mr Thompson? It's still a mystery.'

A gleam came into Spud's eye. 'Maybe *Mr Thompson* is a man of mystery,' he suggested. 'Maybe he's got an assumed identity and really he's someone else entirely – a spy or a criminal or, or – a Mafia boss!'

'No,' laughed Lara. 'I don't believe that for a second!'

I've caught enough baddies in my time, she thought. *I know a goodie when I see one!*

Star shrugged. 'Maybe they've just got the wrong person.'

'That's what Mr Thompson thinks. He's hoping that they'll realize their mistake now and leave him alone,' said Lara.

'Well, I don't think they'll come back in a hurry,' said Spud.

'No,' agreed Lara. 'Although we shouldn't drop our guard just yet.'

She tipped the rest of the fairy cakes into a plastic box and closed the lid. 'Anyway, we've got something else to think about today, haven't we?'

'Yay! The school fete!' woofed Spud. The pups had been looking forward to this for weeks.

'The bouncy castle!' said Star, jumping up and down as if she were already on it.

'And the strawberries and cream!' added Spud, licking his lips.

'And the real fire engine with real fire-fighters!' said Star.

'And the barbecue!' laughed Spud, 'with sausages and burgers and steak and –'

'OK, OK,' laughed Lara. 'Come on, we'd better take these cakes down to the school – the fete will be starting soon.'

Fifteen miles away in the city, Dale was eating his usual breakfast of a Mars bar between two pieces of toast. 'I'm never going back there, Cliff, no way! That place is jinxed!' he said through a mouthful of chocolate and crumbs.

'Yeah, right.' Cliff wasn't listening. He was reading a letter.

'I mean, what was all that with our legs yesterday? We don't know, do we? It was like something from a horror film. I tell you, it's too weird. I've had it with this game. I'm stopping right now.'

'No, you're not, Dale,' said Cliff, looking up calmly, 'and I'll tell you why . . . because this letter is from H in prison and he's given us a lead. Looks like we may have to share the money with him after all, but, hey – we'll still end up with more than ten million smackeroonies each!'

Hugh Higsley-Hogbottom's prison sentence was short to begin with and he'd behaved so well that it was now going to be even shorter. He was polite, helpful and pleasant to everyone. He admitted that he'd 'made a silly mistake' over his taxes, but he seemed so respectable in every other way that all the prison officers agreed they'd never met a more unlikely criminal. They wouldn't have guessed in a million years that H was the mastermind behind a string of international crimes.

So, when H asked one of the officers if he could write a letter to his two children, the officer was happy to provide him with writing paper. He glanced over the note, of course – that was his job – but it never crossed his mind that it could be written in code or that H had been single all his life and wouldn't know a child if it came up and bit him. The prison officer even put H's letter in the postbox himself.

Now Cliff read that letter aloud.

Dear boys,

I hope you're being good while Daddy is away? I just wanted to let you know that I'll be back next week, a little earlier than planned.

I know you were disappointed that we had to cancel our trip to Switzerland, but I promise we'll go as soon as I come back and we'll all have a lovely time.

'Geneva's in Switzerland,' explained Cliff. 'He means we'll go to see that geezer in Geneva – to flog the goods and get the money.'

Mummy tells me you have both been trying very hard at school and asking the teacher lots of questions. That's great, but don't make yourself too much of a nuisance. Teachers don't always know all the answers.

'See what he's doing there, Dale? He's telling us the teacher doesn't know where it is!'

I was very sorry to hear that you've lost your lovely toy horse, the one we got in London before I went away. I know how very precious he is to you.

'Now we know what he means by that, don't we?' said Cliff.

I hope he didn't find his way into the box of things that Mummy gives to charity. Wouldn't it be awful if he got sent to the school fete and was accidentally sold?

But I don't expect that will happen! If you both look very carefully I'm sure you'll find him and then you can bring him with us when we all go off on holiday to Switzerland.

See you next week.
Lots of love,
Daddy

'Why's he calling himself Daddy all of a sudden?' asked Dale.

'Never mind about that, you idiot! The

school is having a fete today. H is telling us he thinks it might be there. He's telling us to go and find it before someone else does!'

'If you say so, bruv,' said Dale slowly, still looking confused. 'But isn't it a bit risky? Someone may have seen us last time we went.'

'Don't worry about that,' said Cliff. 'I've got a plan!'

12. It's Fete!

Everyone in the Cook family was involved in the fete in some way. Mrs Cook was in charge of the bookstall; Mr Cook was helping with the barbecue; Lara was down as a first-aider and Gran had volunteered herself and Ben for the bric-a-brac stall (or 'junk stall' as Mr Cook described it). Star put her name down for the welly tossing – her job was to run and fetch the boots after they'd been thrown – and Sophie had made a big board with pictures of all the teachers when they were babies – anyone who could guess all the teachers from their baby photos would get a prize.

Ollie and Spud had offered to organize a 'Guess the Number of Sweets in the Jar' competition, but when they were trying to assemble it at home, neither of them could resist eating the sweets and so they kept losing

count. In the end, they decided to do a 'Guess the Name of the Teddy' competition instead*.

The school playground was transformed

---

* In case you're wondering, the teddy's name was Vladimir.

with stalls and activities filling every available space and spilling out over the field. Coloured bunting was draped over the buildings, and balloons were tied to the trees. The summery sound of a steel band drifted through the air and, as all the volunteers set about their tasks, the atmosphere was happy and friendly.

Just as the fete was about to begin, Mr Thompson arrived at Gran's bric-a-brac stall. He was carrying a large cardboard box with a one-eared gnome peeping out of the top.

'I found this lot in my garden shed,' he explained. 'The people who used to live in my house must have left it behind and I certainly don't want any of it! I'm afraid it's probably just a load of old rubbish, though.'

'Step this way,' laughed Gran. 'We'll sell it, whatever it is!'

'I hope so,' said Mr Thompson, giving the box to Ben. 'Right, then, I'm off to the "Soak the Teacher" stall – apparently people are willing to pay to chuck wet sponges at my head!'

'Good luck!' laughed Ben.

'Thanks,' said Mr Thompson with a smile. 'At least it's a nice warm day!'

Ben began to unpack Mr Thompson's box while Gran wrote prices on stickers and stuck them on each item. Apart from the gnome there was an old-fashioned kettle; a big yellow vase; a pair of garden shears; a mug with 'I ♥ Disco' on it; a hot-water bottle; a bag of compost and, wrapped in some newspaper at the bottom of the box, an old plate with a rather striking black border and a picture of a flying horse in the middle.

'Ooh, that's rather nice, isn't it?' said Gran, as Ben held up the plate. 'I think we could charge a bit more for that – maybe a fiver? What do you think?'

Ben looked at the plate more closely. It was very unusual. He thought it might be the sort of thing his mum might like – and she had a birthday coming up soon.

'Yes, maybe,' he said, wishing he had more money on him. 'But wait a minute, Gran, I've just got to go and ask Dad something.'

Ben went off to see if he could borrow the money from his dad. He found Mr Cook wearing a white chef's hat and a silly apron, trying not to burn sausages on the barbecue.

In the meantime, more and more people

were flooding into the playground and the stalls were beginning to get busy.

A minute later, Lara came wandering past the stall and gave Gran a friendly wave. *Bric-a-brac's not really my thing*, she thought. *Whack the Rat sounds interesting, though. I wonder what it is?*

Then Lara noticed something out of the corner of her eye. She stopped walking and did a double take. *That plate on Gran's stall . . . it looks a lot like . . . It reminds me of . . . But no, it can't be, that's silly . . .*

Spud came bouncing up to her. 'Come and have a go at this, Ma!' he said excitedly. 'It's not a real rat – just a pair of old socks. Someone drops them down a drainpipe and you have a baseball bat and when they come out you try to whack them before they hit the ground, like this . . .' *WHACK! WHACK!* 'It's great!'

But Lara was trained to act on her suspicions – she couldn't just brush them aside.

'Maybe later, Spud; I've just got to go and check something now . . .'

As Lara trotted off towards the school buildings, Ben came back to the stall with the money he had borrowed from Dad. 'I'd like to buy that plate for Mum's birthday,' he said.

'Oh, that's a lovely idea,' said Gran, wrapping it up again in the newspaper that it came in. 'Now, you don't want it to get broken,' she added. 'So put it out of the way somewhere until it's time to go home.'

Ben looked around for a safe place. *I wonder if I could leave it inside the school*, he thought. *I'll go and ask Mr Thompson.*

Ben found Sophie's teacher peering through a hole in a cardboard wall while a line of children – and one or two of his colleagues – waited to aim wet sponges at him. Lots of people missed their target, but even so, poor Mr Thompson was completely drenched, with water running down his forehead and into his eyes. Somehow he was still managing to smile.

'Excuse me, Mr T,' called Ben, holding up the wrapped plate. 'Would it be OK if I put this in your classroom for a bit? It's china and I don't want it to get broken.'

'Ouf! Phoo!' replied Mr Thompson, as a sponge thrown by a girl of about five caught him squarely on the nose. 'Goodness, Tilly, you can certainly pack a punch! Er, yes, Ben, that's fine. Put it in my desk. It'll be quite safe there. Aargh! Urgh!' he exclaimed as another sponge hit him on the chin. 'Nice shot, Edward! OK, Ollie, you're next!'

Meanwhile Lara had gone straight to the head teacher's office where a group of mums were busy organizing change for the stallholders. They all knew Lara so they weren't surprised when she sat down at the head's computer and turned it on.

Lara typed STOLEN GREEK PLATE into the search box and waited for the computer to link her to the news website she and Sophie had been looking at the day before. This time Lara leant forward and studied the picture more closely.

It was of a medium-sized, reddish-brown-coloured plate with swirly black decorations all round the rim and in the centre, a very distinctive painting of a black horse with huge wings spread out as if it were flying. *That's it!* Lara's eyes were open wide. *That's the plate on Gran's bric-a-brac stall!*

13. The Odd Couple

'I think this fete's going to be a great success!' said Mrs Cook as she handed over the last of the professor's books to a delighted lady physicist. 'I can't believe how many people have come!'

All the children from the school were there with their families, neighbours and friends. Older children who had moved on to secondary school had come back and were marvelling at how small the chairs were in the Year One classroom, and little ones who were still at nursery were brought along to give them an idea of what 'big' school was like.

The teachers had come along too. Some of them, like Mr Thompson, were helping with the stalls, and others were happily buying raffle tickets and drinking cups of tea. Even Mrs

Simpson, who was on maternity leave, came with her teeny tiny baby in a sling. So many girls gathered round to take turns holding little Martha that someone said Mrs Simpson should be charging for every go!

The animal neighbourhood watch team were well represented – several of the bigger dogs, including Potter, had gathered around the barbecue area and Scottie had stationed himself permanently under the table where the cakes were being sold.

In the general crush one couple in particular didn't really stand out, even though, on closer inspection, they did look a bit odd. The man was tall and thin with a ginger beard and thick-rimmed glasses. He was wearing a panama hat pulled well over his eyes. The woman was very solidly built, to say the least, and was wearing a tight red dress with white spots that looked like it might burst at the seams at any minute. She had long, luxuriant blonde hair, rather like Miss Piggy's, and was wearing big sunglasses and a lot of red lipstick. She had a large white handbag and matching shoes. The heels of the shoes weren't particularly high, but she seemed to have trouble walking in them.

'I feel completely ridiculous,' she muttered
to her partner in a surprisingly gruff voice. 'Are
you sure I can get away with this, bruv?'

'You look lovely, Dale!' said the man out of
the corner of his mouth, keeping his eyes fixed

straight ahead. 'Our own mother wouldn't recognize you. Come on now, gorgeous, we've got to get on with the job.'

Dale and Cliff made their way to the bric-a-brac stall and started looking through the contents.

'May I help?' asked Gran pleasantly. 'Are you looking for anything in particular?'

'Erm, yes,' said Cliff. 'We're looking for a plate – er – we're going to buy a cake, you see, and we want something to put it on.'

'Ooh, well, we've got one or two nice plates,' said Gran. 'There's a pretty little one here with flowers on it. What about this?'

Cliff looked at Dale. 'We were looking for something a bit bigger and a bit more – er – classical-looking, weren't we, dear?'

'Yahs,' said blonde Dale in a high-pitched and surprisingly posh voice. 'In darker colours, like – erm – red and black.'

'Oh, that's a pity,' said Gran, 'because we did have a plate just like that. Really interesting it was; it had some kind of animal on it, I think. But it's just been sold. My grandson bought it, actually – it's his mum's birthday soon, you see, and –' But her two customers weren't listening.

They had turned away and were having an urgent muttered conversation.

'Excuse me! How much for those antlers?' Gran turned away to serve another customer.

'Some dratted kid has bought it!' snarled Dale.

'Well, we'd better find him quickly, then,' snapped Cliff. 'Ask the old dear what he looks like.'

'I can't, she'll suspect something.'

'Yes, you can – you're a *woman,* don't forget; you're meant to be *interested* in kids. Go on!' Cliff gave Dale a little push so that he tottered slightly in his white court shoes as he turned back to the stall.

'How lahvely to have a grandson!' he said in his strange new voice. 'What does he look . . . erm . . . Does he look like you at all?'

Gran smiled. Her grandchildren were her specialist subject. 'No, not really, bless him, although I like to think he's got my blue eyes. His hair's like his dad's, though, not like mine at all.'

'Ask her what it's like,' hissed Cliff.

'Oh, really?' said Dale. 'Is it – er – curly or straight?'

'It's pretty straight, really; mine's always had a natural curl – mind you, my sister's hair has always been straight, so maybe he takes after her.'

Dale glanced back at Cliff and rolled his eyes. Cliff tapped pointedly at his clothes. Dale looked blank. Then he had a brainwave.

'And, er, I suppose he's very fashion-conscious, is he, your grandson? What sort of clothes does he wear?'

Gran laughed. 'They all are, aren't they, these days. He's a great one for . . . oh, excuse me, I must just help that lady with those golf clubs!'

Dale turned back to Cliff. 'Hopeless. The kid's got blue eyes and straight hair along with half the other kids at the fete,' he muttered.

At that moment Ollie, who was doing star jumps on the bouncy castle, shouted loudly, 'Gran! Gran! Look at this! Watch me!'

'Oh yes, dear. Very nice!' called Gran, as Ollie carried on jumping. She turned to the woman she was serving. 'That's my grandson,' she said proudly. 'He's always so full of beans!'

Dale and Cliff looked at one another and smiled.

'Bingo!' said Cliff.

14. Hunting for Ben

Back in the head teacher's office, Lara's mind was racing as she stared at the crime report on the computer screen. She didn't know how it had got there, but she knew there was a priceless antiquity lying unrecognized among all the junk on Gran's stall. *Anyone could buy it – or it might get damaged – or broken. Aaargh! I've got to act fast!*

The Spy Dog quickly clicked on PRINT and waited impatiently as the paper shuffled slowly out of the head's rather elderly printer, then she grabbed the paper in her mouth and ran out of the building.

'Oh, there you are, Lara!' Sophie came running up to meet her. 'I've been looking for you everywhere! Do you want to come and see me have my face painted?'

I wish I could, Sophie, but I'm on an urgent mission – and maybe you can help! Lara showed the article to Sophie, tapping it meaningfully with her paw. Then she started to pull Sophie towards Gran's stall. *Come on, Sophie, follow me. When you see the plate, you'll get the idea!*

Sophie quickly realized that Lara had something on her mind. 'What's the matter? Is it something to do with this stolen plate?' she asked. Lara nodded vigorously.

They reached the stall and Lara started hunting for the plate. *It was just over there beside that yellow vase . . . Oh no! Where is it? Someone must have bought it while I was away!*

'Gran, have you seen a plate like this, by any chance?' asked Sophie, showing Gran the picture.

'I can't see very well without my glasses, dear,' said Gran. 'But it looks a lot like the one Mr Thompson brought in with all that other stuff he found in his garden shed.'

Lara's brain whirred into overdrive. So this was the solution to the mystery that had been bugging her for days! All the different pieces of the puzzle suddenly fell into place.

Now I get it! Those two crooks are after that plate.

That's why they searched Mr Thompson's house, and the school, and that's why they threatened him. And Mr T had no idea! Of course, it all makes perfect sense!

Now there was just one problem – and Sophie was on to it straight away, 'Where is the plate now, Gran?' she asked.

'Oh, Ben bought it to give to your mum for her birthday. Wasn't that nice? He's gone off to put it somewhere safe.'

Phew! thought Lara. *Thank goodness! Now we just have to find Ben and then tell the police.*

'It's funny . . .' went on Gran, 'everyone seems to be interested in that plate today. Some other people were looking for one like that too. I told them it was sold, of course. Nice couple, they were, really chatty – and interested in Ben as well. I must say you meet some lovely people at these school dos.'

Lara felt the fur on her back standing on end. *Yikes! Those two must be the crooks – who else would be asking about that particular plate? And Gran's gone and told them that Ben's got it! They'll be after him now – and they're hardened criminals who'll stop at nothing!*

Sophie saw the alarm on Lara's face. 'It's OK,'

she said. 'We'll split up and look for Ben. He can't be far away. I'll go this way; you go that way, Lara.'

Lara began to hurry through the crowded playground, looking and listening carefully to everyone around her. As she got to the bouncy castle she noticed Ollie deep in conversation with two strangers – a bearded man in a hat and a heavily built blonde woman in a spotty dress. The pair didn't match the pups' descriptions of the baddies, but Lara's training still put her on full alert.

There's something odd about that woman. What is it? Her hair looks strange . . . and she's standing in a funny way . . .

Lara moved closer so she could listen in on their conversation. She casually sniffed the ground, deliberately avoiding eye contact so they wouldn't notice her. *That's the advantage of being a dog. People don't realize you're listening!*

'Oh no, it wasn't me!' Ollie was saying. 'You must mean my big brother, Ben. He's twelve. He always gets Mum a present for her birthday. I usually just make her something – she likes that – or last year I gave her a bunch of –'

'Yeah, yeah, we get it,' interrupted the man

rudely. 'So, where's your brother now? Has he still got the plate? Or has he given it to your mum already?'

'No, he definitely wouldn't have done that,' explained Ollie patiently, 'because her birthday's not till next Thursday, I think – or maybe it's Wednesday, I'm not quite sure. My dad says –'

The blonde woman's huge fists were clenched. She leant forward over Ollie in a menacing way, but the bearded man put out his arm to stop her. Lara moved up beside them and gave a low growl. *Don't even think about it . . .!*

'Look, kid, we don't have much time,' said the man grimly. 'Just tell us where your brother is RIGHT NOW!'

'Oh, OK!' said Ollie, a little taken aback. 'Well, last time I saw him he was going off to put something in Mr Thompson's desk. If you're quick he might still be in the classroom now. It's Class Five,' he added helpfully.

'Result!' the woman shouted in an oddly masculine voice, punching the air. 'Come on, bruv, let's go, go, GO!'

As the pair turned, Lara got a good look at them. *Yikes! That isn't a woman at all – it's one of*

*the crooks in a dress! And the man in the beard's the
other one!*

Dale and Cliff knew they were hot on the trail
now. All they had to do was get the plate from
a twelve-year-old kid – and how hard could
that be? They hurled themselves through the
crowd, knocking over the coconut shy and

taking a short cut straight through Year Three's display of country dancing.

Dale's clothes made it hard for him to run, but he pulled up his dress above his knees and did his best. As he pushed past the cake stall he turned his ankle over and only saved himself by putting his hand smack in the middle of a Victoria sponge.

'Must be an emergency,' remarked the vicar. 'That poor lady is certainly in a hurry.'

But Lara was faster – and she'd worked out a quicker way to the classroom. Spy Dogs are trained to keep calm and think clearly in any situation. As she sprinted round the edge of the stalls towards the open classroom window, Lara ran through her priorities in order. *One – make sure Ben is safe; two – get the plate back; three – catch the criminals.*

Lara ran past Sophie and Mr Thompson, seeing them in a blur. She could tell that Sophie was telling her teacher about the situation because he was staring at Lara's printout and looking rather pale, but Lara had no time to stop. She clambered in through the open classroom window, desperate to get there ahead of the two criminals.

15. The Precious Parcel

Dale and Cliff burst through the classroom door like two bad cowboys entering a saloon. The room was cool, shady and perfectly still. Through the open window could be heard the faint sound of accordion music and the murmur of distant voices.

'The kid's gone,' said Cliff. 'Good. We don't want any inconvenient witnesses, do we? Now where's he put that old plate?'

'Should be in the teacher's desk,' said Dale, crossing the room. 'There's something here – it's wrapped in newspaper.' He opened the paper and glanced inside. 'Yessss! We've got it at last! Ten million euros' worth of old china equals our ticket to a life of luxury! Take a good look, bruv, because I'm holding our futures in my hand!'

'Well, don't go waving it about, you idiot,'

said Cliff. 'If you break that plate now I swear I'll break *you* – into tiny pieces with my bare hands! We're gonna guard this little baby with our lives – until we've passed it over to that Swiss geezer and got the dosh.'

He took the parcel from Dale and put it carefully into Dale's large white handbag. 'Now be careful, right? No sudden movements.'

'Got it,' said Dale. 'Come on, let's get out of here. My feet are killing me.'

The two men turned, only to find Mr Thompson walking through the classroom door.

'Can I help you?' he asked pleasantly.

Underneath a table in the corner of the classroom, Lara and Ben were crouching motionless. Lara had decided the best way to protect Ben was to hide him from the villains. She'd bundled him under the table moments before Dale and Cliff arrived. Ben was surprised, of course, but he always trusted Lara and, as he listened to the men's conversation, he began to understand why she had been so insistent. When Mr Thompson came in they both stiffened with fear.

Oh no, Mr T, no heroics, please! thought Lara. *These men are dangerous!*

The baddies weren't pleased to see him, either. 'Just play along,' muttered Cliff to Dale under his breath. 'Remember, he doesn't know who we are.'

'Good afternoon,' he said politely to Mr Thompson. 'My wife and I were just, um, having a look around the school. We're thinking of sending our little boy here, aren't we, dear?'

'Yahs,' said Dale, adopting his posh lady's voice again. 'Yahs, that's right, dahling.'

'I see,' said Mr Thompson. 'Well, I'm awfully sorry, but would you mind letting me have a look in your handbag? Just a security check, you know.'

'No way, José!' said Dale, clutching the bag firmly to his well-padded chest.

Cliff laughed nervously. 'Oh dear, you know what ladies are like about their handbags!' he said to Mr Thompson in a man-to-man sort of way. 'I'm sure I don't know *what* they keep in them!'

Mr Thompson wasn't fooled. He strolled casually over to his desk and looked inside. Then he spun round and faced the crooks. 'OK, I'm on to you. Give me that plate, right NOW,' he said in his fiercest voice. The one that usually made even the naughtiest Year Five quake.

Oh no! thought Lara. *Now, he's done it!*

In the blink of an eye, Dale had grabbed Mr Thompson's arm and twisted it hard behind his back. Mr Thompson struggled, but Dale was far too strong.

'So you knew about the plate all along, did you?' growled Dale. 'Well, you're too late. We've got it now – and we've got you too.'

Lara knew she had to do something. Hoping Ben wouldn't follow her, she came out from under the table, growling and barking fiercely. Dale's hand went into the pocket of his spotty dress and he pulled out his gun. 'Shall I shut the dog up, bruv?' he snarled, aiming at Lara's head. Lara knew she was beaten.

'It's OK,' said Mr Thompson desperately. 'She's a friendly dog, really, aren't you, Lara? She won't hurt you – or bark any more, will you, girl?' Mr Thompson looked at Lara imploringly, begging her to save her own life.

Huh! I've got to act stupid or we'll both be for it, thought Lara. She forced herself to wag her tail. Then she lay down and cocked her head on one side, trying to look as friendly as she could.

Cliff snorted. 'Stupid mutt! What kind of

dog is that? Not much use as a guard dog, is it? No use to anyone.' Lara's eyes narrowed, but she kept pretending.

But Dale remembered the last time they'd been in that classroom and the strange thing that had happened with those puppies – they had seemed friendly enough as well.

'Come on, bruv,' he said. 'Let's get going before anything else happens.'

The two men positioned themselves firmly on either side of Mr Thompson. 'I'll take the gun,' said Cliff. 'You look after the handbag – and be very, *very* careful with it, bruv – remember what I said.'

Cliff put the gun in his pocket, but held it so that it nudged against Mr Thompson's ribs. 'Right, you, get moving – you're coming with us!'

The three walked together down the corridor as if they were the best of friends. Lara followed close behind. After they'd left the classroom, Ben crawled out from under the table and started to follow too.

I can't raise the alarm, he thought desperately. *They might open fire. What can I do? What can anyone do?*

16. Hair Raising!

As Lara meekly followed Dale, Cliff and Mr Thompson down the corridor, she tried to calculate what might happen next. *They won't just let him go, that's for sure. He knows too much. Their car must be parked in the road outside. I'm guessing they'll take him with them. Ben and I can raise the alarm once they've gone, but it may be too late. Too late for Mr Thompson, that is . . .*

'Oh, hello there, Mr T! Glad to see you've managed to get dried off at last.' A group of parents were walking down the corridor.

'I have to say you're a really good sport,' said one of the dads. 'I wouldn't fancy doing something like that, would you?' He included Cliff and Dale in his friendly smile.

Dale just scowled. Cliff nudged Mr Thompson with the barrel of his gun.

'Well, thanks, um, yes, sorry, got to dash!' said Mr Thompson rather wildly, and the three men carried on walking.

'Don't try any funny business,' muttered Cliff in Mr Thompson's ear. 'No winks, no nods, no coded messages. If someone talks to you, act natural – but keep moving.'

'OK,' said Mr Thompson, 'but it's tricky. People will expect me to stop and chat.'

'Well, you can't, OK?' said Cliff. 'We've got places to go. Just do as I say – or else . . .'

This is unreal, thought Lara as they made their way out into the playground. There they were in the sunshine among all those friendly faces and no one but Lara and Ben realized that, at any minute, something truly terrible could happen. *There are literally hundreds of people here who could help us – if only they knew what was going on!*

The trio were heading towards the school gates now. In less than a minute they'd be gone. Suddenly the head teacher appeared from round the front of the parked fire engine. 'Oh, Mr Thompson, I'm so sorry to bother you, but could you come with me to my office for a moment? I've got a little problem with the safe.'

For a moment the word 'safe' made Cliff's eyes light up, but then he remembered that however much money was in the school safe, it would be nothing compared to the money they'd get from selling the contents of Dale's handbag. He gave Mr Thompson a meaningful look.

'N-no, sorry,' said Mr Thompson. 'I'm . . . I'm just showing these parents round. I can't stop.' He started to walk on, but the head teacher planted herself firmly in front of them. 'I don't believe we've met,' she said, holding out her hand to Dale. 'I'm Miss Lancaster, the school head.'

Dale was forced to release his grip on Mr Thompson for a second to shake hands. Remembering his disguise, Dale answered in his lady's voice. 'Charmed, I'm sure,' he said. 'I'm, er, Mrs . . . Gun.' Cliff looked at him sharply. 'I mean Gum, yes, Gum. Ha! Ha! Silly name, isn't it? And this is my husband – er, well, oh, Mr Gum, of course!'

Now Miss Lancaster held out her hand to Cliff, who had to do some awkward manoeuvring to switch the gun into his other hand. Mr Thompson wondered if he should make a break for freedom, but he didn't dare. *It's just too risky, especially with all these people about.*

'And who's your son or daughter?' asked the head pleasantly.

Cliff decided he'd better take over the talking. 'He's not at your school yet. We're prospective parents, you see. Mr Thompson is just showing us round, aren't you?' Another dig in Mr Thompson's ribs.

If I survive this I'll be black and blue! thought Mr T.

Meanwhile Lara had suddenly had an idea. Leaving the unlikely looking threesome to talk to Miss Lancaster, she raced towards the 'Hook the Duck' stall, where children were trying to pick up little plastic ducks using long sticks with hooks on the end. Lara grabbed one of the sticks from a small boy and ran off with it in her mouth. *Sorry! But this is a matter of life or death!*

Ben watched her in surprise. *What on earth is Lara going to do with that?* he wondered.

Lara knew exactly what she was going to do. She was going to unmask the villains – using an element of surprise. *It's a gamble, but I've got to try it.*

As the conversation with the head teacher continued, Lara climbed up the back of the parked fire engine and on to its roof, carrying the hooked stick in her mouth. Then she crawled over the roof and positioned herself just above where Dale was standing.

Ben realized in a flash what Lara was trying to do. 'Let me help!' he hissed and began to scramble up the back of the fire engine too.

Ben and Lara had been fishing together many times, but never quite like this. Lara knew that Ben was an expert with a fishing rod – and his aim would be more accurate than hers. She passed him the stick and he gently lowered the hook over Dale's blonde wig and then, with a quick flick of his wrist, pulled it right off Dale's head and landed it on top of the engine.

Dale was completely taken by surprise. He spun round so fast that his sunglasses fell off too. 'Oi!' he shouted in his normal voice. 'Who's had me wig?'

Cliff was surprised too. He jumped sideways, taking the gun out of his pocket so that, for a split second, it was aimed at Miss Lancaster instead.

Suddenly it was clear to the head teacher and

everyone else nearby that Dale was not a
tubby blonde woman at all, but a very tough
man in a dress, and that the man with the

rather fake-looking ginger beard was holding an all-too-real-looking gun. Miss Lancaster screamed and Mr Thompson started to try to break free.

Dale was panicking, but Cliff was icy calm. He held the gun so it was pointing at Mr Thompson's head.

'Get in the fire engine, Dale,' he said. 'There's been a change of plan.'

17. Where's the Fire?

When Miss Lancaster agreed that the fire crew could come to the school fete she understood that they might have to leave in a hurry. She knew that the engine had to be parked facing the gates and that there must be no obstructions in its path to the road in case of an emergency. But she never imagined she would see it speeding off with one of her best young teachers sitting inside, sandwiched between two dangerous armed criminals. And even in her wildest dreams, she wouldn't have thought that there would be a twelve-year-old boy and a black and white Spy Dog riding on top of the roof.

'Stop! Stop! That's my brother!' shouted Sophie.

'And our mum!' woofed Spud and Star.

Sophie and the pups ran after the fire engine as it accelerated away, but they knew it was useless. By the time they reached the road, the engine was already out of sight. All they could

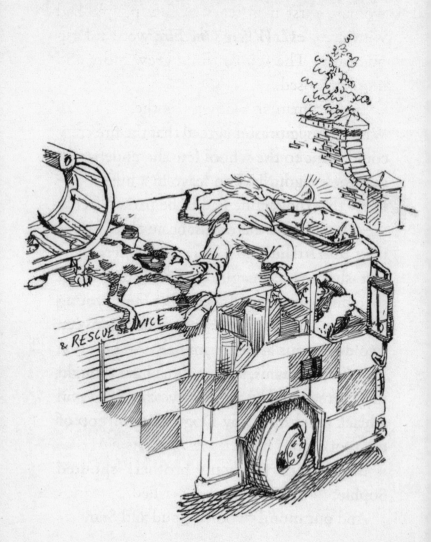

hear was the wail of its siren as it disappeared into the distance.

After a moment of shocked silence, everyone in the playground began to talk and shout. One woman burst into tears. A few people had witnessed everything; others were asking questions. The whole thing grew more and more confused.

'It was a man, in women's clothes!'

'He had a gun!'

'Take cover, everyone!'

'They've got Mr Thompson!'

'Call the police!'

'Was that Ben Cook on the roof?'

'Where's the fire?'

'Evacuate the school!'

'Mr Thompson's gone mad. He's dressed up in women's clothes and stolen a fire engine!"

The fire crew were all enjoying strawberries and cream in the marquee when they heard the siren. They dropped their bowls and stampeded across the grass in their heavy boots, but they got there much too late.

Mr and Mrs Cook were horrified. Mr Cook

wanted to jump in his car and chase after the engine – but then he remembered he'd left the car at home.

'Don't worry,' said Sophie, trying to sound reassuring. 'Remember, Lara's trained to deal with every sort of danger. She'll make sure that Ben's OK.'

'That's right,' said Spud to Star. 'A Spy Dog knows no fear!'

But Ollie hugged Spud and gave Sophie's hand a little squeeze. He knew they were just as anxious as everybody else.

At the wheel of the fire engine, Dale was having the time of his life.

'Yeee-ha!' he shouted as he floored the accelerator. 'I've always wanted to drive one of these babies!' It was his ideal vehicle. With the siren screaming and the lights flashing, every car on the road stopped to let him through. People even pulled over on to the verge and waved him past. 'I love it! I could drive all day!' he yelled above the noise.

'Well, you can't,' said Cliff crossly. 'Because the cops will be after us very soon and we're not exactly inconspicuous in this thing, are we?

Turn that blooming siren off for a start.' Reluctantly Dale did as he was told.

'Why did you have to go and lose your wig like that?' said Cliff angrily. 'We could have slipped out of there with no one any the wiser. Now we're in a right mess.'

Dale frowned. 'Yeah, I don't know how that happened,' he said. 'Must've been the wind, I suppose. Can't say I'm sorry it's gone, though, it was really itchy.' He ran his hand over his bristly head. 'So, where to now, bruv? What's the plan?'

Dale glanced at Mr Thompson. 'Drive to the lake. Not a lot of people go there, but there's a car park where we should be able to find ourselves a nice new motor. Then the cops won't know what we're driving and we can leave the fire engine behind.'

'What about the teacher?'

'I think we'll leave him behind as well, if you know what I mean,' said Cliff in a nasty voice.

'What *do* you mean?' asked Mr Thompson.

'Did I ask you to speak?' snarled Cliff, his finger tapping the trigger. Mr Thompson decided it might be best if he kept quiet.

Cliff found a bit of rope in the back of the

cab and tied Mr Thompson's wrists tightly together. 'I'm not taking any chances with you,' he said.

None of the men had any idea that they were carrying two extra passengers. As soon as the fire engine started to move, Ben and Lara had climbed on to the ladder on the roof and clung on to it, one in front of the other. As the engine thundered out of the village, the wind rushed past them, blowing Lara's ears flat and lifting Ben's body up and away from the ladder as if he were bodyboarding on air. Lara looked round anxiously. *Hold on tight, Ben! Don't get blown away.*

Lara did her best to wedge her paws underneath the ladder's rungs. *Yikes! We're going much too fast for these roads!* she thought. *And it's a long way down!*

Then Dale stamped on the brakes and made a last-minute left-hand turn. Ben tumbled forward on top of Lara and they both slid sharply to the right. Lara's paws lost their grip. She scrabbled desperately at the shiny red paintwork, scratching it with her claws as she tried to regain her hold – but it was too slippery.

'Lara! No!' Ben wailed and stretched out an arm to try to grab her. He leant over as far as he could, but Lara was tumbling fast.

I'm a goner! Lara caught sight of the road surface flashing past below. Ben stretched his arm as far as it would go and just managed to catch her last back leg. As soon as his hand closed round her, he pulled as hard as he could.

Youch! That hurts – but never mind! I'm still alive!

But Lara's weight and the force of gravity were against them. 'I can't pull you back, but I can stop you from falling!' puffed Ben. *But for how long?* he wondered. *My arm feels like it's coming out of its socket!*

The fire engine thundered on with Lara dangling dangerously over the edge.

'There's another turning ahead!' shouted Ben. He knew this road. It led to Nightingale Lake, a local beauty spot. The Cook family sometimes went for walks there at weekends. 'If we turn right, you'll get thrown back towards the ladder. Get ready!'

Please, turn right! Please! thought Ben.

Sure enough, Dale swerved violently to the right. Ben kept his grip on Lara and she slid back to the left and towards the ladder again.

Phew! Thanks, Ben! Lara wove her paws between the ladder's rungs. *That was a bit too close for comfort!*

Lara knew that they were both in danger. *I can't let this go on*, she thought. *One of us could fall off at any minute. Somehow I've got to make the driver stop – but how?* She thought back to the old days of her Spy Dog training. *What would the professor suggest in a situation like this?*

A picture of the professor's smiling face popped into Lara's mind – and suddenly she had an idea.

18. Nightingale Lake

As the fire engine sped on, Lara turned and began to point urgently towards the buttoned pocket at the front of Ben's cargo trousers.

Ben looked mystified. 'I haven't got any money, Lara,' he shouted. 'I spent it all on that plate!'

Lara shook her head and kept on pointing. *Come on, Ben, think! What might be useful at a time like this?*

'You want something from my pocket?' said Ben. Lara nodded. Ben still looked puzzled, then light dawned. 'Oh, d'you mean the professor's black-out capsule?' he yelled. 'That's brilliant, Lara!' He quickly unbuttoned his pocket. 'Yes, I've still got it – here it is!'

Yessss! Lara leant back and took the capsule from Ben carefully in her mouth. Then just as carefully she began to crawl along the ladder towards the front of the fire engine. The road was getting narrower as they neared the lake and even Cliff was forced to drive a bit more slowly. As Lara edged forward, Ben crawled along behind her.

'It's OK, Lara!' he said. 'I'll hold your back legs so you don't fall.'

Thanks, mate! You could be a Spy Boy yet, you know! You're certainly the best friend a Spy Dog could ever have!

Lara had reached the front of the fire engine now and slid forward on her stomach so that her head and front legs were almost dangling over the top of the windscreen. *I mustn't let anyone see me! I want this to be a big surprise!*

SPLAT! With a flick of her head Lara threw the capsule right into the middle of the windscreen. A moment later the screen was totally black. Dale couldn't see a thing. He jammed on the brakes and brought the fire engine skidding to an emergency stop. Lara and Ben were braced for it and managed to keep their positions on the roof. Ben stifled the urge to cheer and Lara turned and gave him a high-five. *This fire engine isn't going anywhere in a hurry!*

Lara and Ben crawled to the back of the roof

and slid soundlessly down on to the grass. They flattened themselves against the vehicle, hoping they wouldn't be seen. Cliff and Dale jumped out of the cab pulling Mr Thompson with them. Cliff had taken off his beard and glasses, but was still holding the gun; Dale was clutching the precious plate inside the white handbag.

'What just happened then?' asked Dale, staring at the windscreen.

'Never mind about that!' said Cliff. 'Listen!'

They had stopped just before a bridge high up above the lake. The whole area was surrounded by woodland and very peaceful. The only obvious noise was the cooing of a wood pigeon in a nearby tree, but far away in the distance, there was also the faint but unmistakeable sound of a police car's siren.

'We'll have to leg it,' said Cliff urgently.

'What about him?' said Dale, nodding at Mr Thompson.

'I think he wants to go for a swim, don't you?' said Cliff.

'No!' shouted Mr Thompson as Cliff pushed him roughly towards the edge of the bridge. Dale put down the handbag carefully on the grass and went to stand beside his brother.

'Come on now, teacher, don't argue with the man with the gun. It might be a long way down, but I bet that water's lovely!'

Ben and Lara peered round the fire engine in horror. Ben was just about to run out and intervene, but Lara barred his way.

No, Ben. Leave this to me!

Lara broke cover and darted silently towards the handbag. She pulled out the plate from its wrapping and, remembering a move she'd used many times with the pups at home, hurled it just like a Frisbee towards the men.

The plate twisted in an arc through the air and headed straight for Cliff's hand. The criminal looked round for a split second and couldn't believe his eyes. He didn't have time to react. The flying plate hit the gun and knocked it straight out of his hand and down into the lake below. Then, after it had hit its target, the plate crash-landed into the side of the bridge and smashed and splintered into a hundred tiny pieces.

Everybody gasped.

Mr Thompson was the first to move. He broke away from the criminals and raced towards Lara. Cliff and Dale didn't even try to stop him. They were both staring in horror at the pieces of china at their feet.

'Millions and millions of euros, that plate was worth,' said Cliff slowly. 'Millions and millions . . .'

Dale bent to pick up one of the tiny fragments. For a moment it looked like he was going to cry.

Then Cliff snapped into action. The police car was drawing nearer by the second.

'Come on, bruv!' he ordered. 'We've lost the money, but we can still get away! Follow me!'

The two men sprinted across the bridge and down a steep footpath that led to the edge of the water. This time Cliff kicked off his shoes and tucked his spotty dress into his underpants so he could run more easily.

Shall I chase them? thought Lara. But then she had a better idea.

As Ben quickly untied Mr Thompson's hands, Lara grabbed a stick in her mouth and levered open the compartment in the side of the engine where the fire hoses were kept.

'Great idea, Lara!' laughed Mr Thompson. Together they unfurled a hose and Mr T grabbed its nozzle. Cliff and Dale had just arrived at the edge of the lake as Ben and Lara turned on the water supply. Gallons of water began to surge through the hose and Mr Thompson aimed the powerful jet straight at the criminals' knees. It knocked them sideways, hurling them up into the air and then down into the lake.

At that moment the police car drew up with a screech of tyres, and three armed police officers raced down the path to the water's edge.

'Armed police!' they shouted. 'Swim back here or we'll shoot!'

Cliff and Dale knew they were beaten. Coughing and spluttering and covered in waterweed, they both swam slowly back to the shore.

'Hope you enjoyed your dip,' said one of the officers. 'There won't be any swimming where you're going, that's for sure.'

19. The School Assembly

Every year there was a special school assembly after the fete to thank those who had taken part and to announce how much money had been raised. This year the school hall was packed. Everyone in the village had come to find out exactly what else had happened that day.

Mr and Mrs Cook were there with Gran, and Ben had the morning off school and was sitting in the front row with Lara and the pups. Sophie and Ollie were with their classmates, and Mr Thompson was sitting on the stage behind Miss Lancaster.

'First of all,' said the head, 'I want to thank all of you who so generously gave up your time, your skills – and of course your hard-earned cash. We raised a record-breaking sum and we'll be able to buy some much-needed computer equipment for the school and also make a large donation to our local charities . . .' She went on to mention the different amounts of money raised by various stalls and to thank certain people by name. Everyone clapped politely, but no one was really listening.

'But, as you know, there was a little more excitement on Saturday than any of us would have wished for. So many rumours have been flying around that I think it's high time I pass you over to Mr Thompson so he can explain what really happened and put the record straight.' Mr Thompson stood up. 'And I'd just like to say,' added Miss Lancaster, 'on behalf of everyone, that we are all *very* pleased to see you – and Ben – safe and well here this morning!'

'Hear, hear!' said a voice and everyone began to clap.

Mr Thompson smiled as he took the microphone and began to tell the whole story. When he got to the bit where Lara rescued him by using the plate to knock the gun out of the criminal's hand, Mr Thompson sounded quite emotional. 'I expect you can imagine how I felt,' he said. 'I have never been more grateful in my life!'

Everyone clapped again and some people cheered. Spud and Star woofed loudly. Lara looked modestly at the floor.

Mr Thompson carried on to the end of the story. 'So, you'll all be glad to know that not only are the two villains safely under arrest,' he said, 'but also the police have discovered the mastermind behind this and a string of other unsolved crimes. They may also be able to recover many other stolen goods.'

'And speaking of stolen goods,' Mr Thompson went on. 'Even though human life is worth more than any piece of pottery, however precious — and my life's certainly worth a lot to me! — I have to say that when I saw that plate lying smashed on the ground, I couldn't help feeling just a tiny bit sad that such a beautiful and important piece of Greek history was now lost forever.'

He paused and looked around him, smiling. 'But, ladies and gentleman, boys and girls — I need not have worried! Because when Lara went ahead of the thieves into my classroom that afternoon, she had just enough time to swap the stolen plate for another one – a plate made by Sophie as part of our class project.

'Lara wrapped Sophie's plate in newspaper and put it in my desk. She took a chance that the crooks wouldn't notice the difference – and she was right!'

Everyone gasped, even Miss Lancaster.

'So,' smiled Mr Thompson, 'the plate that Lara used to save my life was made by Sophie just three days ago, and the one that was made by an ancient Greek potter three *thousand years* ago was sitting safely in my classroom all along – and now it's back in the British Museum where it belongs!'

The room went into uproar. No one had expected this! Everyone stood up and clapped, cheered and whistled. The pups jumped about in the air and Mrs Cook gave Lara a hug.

Mr Thompson beckoned Lara up on to the stage and Miss Lancaster put a garland of flowers round her neck. Then the teachers called Ben, Sophie, Ollie and the pups on to the stage as well.

The pups' tails were wagging so hard it looked like their whole bodies were wagging. 'Our mum's a Super Dog!' said Spud.

'She's a Super-Super Spy Dog!' said Star. 'And I hope we'll be just like her when we grow up.'

As the clapping and cheering subsided, Miss Lancaster took the microphone again. 'There's just one more thing,' she said. 'In all the excitement we forgot to announce the winner of the raffle. As you know the prize is a relaxing two-day break at a country house hotel and spa, and I'm pleased to say the winner is – Mrs Cook!'

Everyone laughed.

'Just the thing for your birthday!' said Gran.

'Yes,' said Mrs Cook. 'I think we all need to relax for a day or two, before Lara gets involved in another adventure!'

Turn the page for a sneak peek from . . .

SPY PUPS
TREASURE QUEST

1. Double Trouble

'Don't be sad, Lara,' soothed Ollie, stroking his dog behind the ear. 'You've still got two puppies left and Mum says we can keep them.'

'And the others have gone to brilliant homes,' added Sophie, trying but failing to sound chirpy.

Lara lay with her head on her paws. She knew the children were right but it didn't stop the pain in her heart. *Hopefully time will heal it*, she thought. *It's so difficult when my babies leave home.* She watched Spud and Star play-fighting. *Bags of energy*, she thought. 'Calm down, you two,' she woofed. 'Why don't you play Scrabble or Monopoly or something a bit calmer?' Her two remaining puppies looked at their mum as if she was mad. Chasing each other around the lounge was much more fun.

Lara reflected on the last four months. *It's been a hectic time*, she smiled. *Becoming a mum of seven, instilling some discipline, getting the pups house-trained and teaching them some of the spy-dog basics. Phew! No wonder I'm always exhausted.*

Lara watched as Spud sat on his sister, squeezing the breath out of her.

'Gotcha!' he barked.

'No, you haven't,' she woofed, twisting away and nipping him on the backside. 'Too slow, bro!'

Lara always knew that most of the pups would be adopted. Dad had explained it to her shortly after she found she was pregnant. And Lara understood – the house just wasn't big enough to keep them all. Her mission was to find good homes. Each time there was an adoption her tummy churned with happiness and sadness. She was delighted with the new owners. Her eldest daughter, Bessie, had gone to a farmer. He had other dogs and Lara knew they were well cared for. Bessie had a good life ahead of her as a working farm dog. *Perfect*, thought the retired spy dog. *One sorted, seven to go!*

Toddy and Mr G had gone as a pair, hand selected by the police as sniffer dogs. Lara approved. *They are both lively boys,* she thought, *so they will get all the action they crave. And maybe do some good for the world too.* Lara reflected on her spy-dog days and shuddered at the thought of all the baddies she'd stopped, especially her arch-enemy, Mr Big. *I sniffed out his evil drugs empire and put him behind bars.*

Twice! Maybe my boys will do the same, she hoped.

Lara had a particular soft spot for Britney. She was the youngest – *a whole nineteen minutes younger than Bessie* – and quietest of the litter. *Seen but not heard*, thought Lara. *Definitely not police dog material but very clever and a great companion. Being selected as a guide dog was perfect*, reflected Lara. *She'll be the top of her class and there will be one very lucky owner!*

TinTin was always going to be a handful. He was a rather strange-looking pup. His brothers and sisters were black and white but TinTin was splodged with brown patches. His energy levels were off the scale and his tail never stopped wagging. He was sometimes a little overenthusiastic. His shaggy coat made him the perfect choice to go and work with his granddad, Leo, in Scotland. TinTin had enrolled to be a mountain rescue dog and his mum couldn't be more proud. *A very worthwhile career. And I know his granddad will take good care of him.*

Lara watched her two remaining puppies chasing around the table legs. *Good homes, all*

of them, she thought. *And I'm lucky that the Cook family have let me keep these two.*

'Mum, what's for lunch?' asked Spud, taking a break from annoying his sister.

Lara sniffed the air. 'Spaghetti hoops ... peas,' she woofed, '. . . and sausages.'

'And when's it lunchtime?' yapped her son. 'I'm starving.'

'You're always starving!' Lara glanced at the clock. 'Half an hour,' she replied.

'How long's half an hour?' asked Spud.

'Not long,' she barked, rising wearily to her feet and stretching. 'Just long enough to work on those times tables before we eat!'

2. Cat Burglar

Lunch was cleared away and it was time for the pups' afternoon snooze. Lara loved living with the Cooks. *It's not all out adventure and excitement like when I was a spy dog,* she thought, *but we've certainly had more than our fair share of scrapes.*

Lara had adopted the Cooks when they'd turned up at the RSPCA. Before then she'd been working as a spy dog for the Secret Service – the name LARA on her tag actually stood for 'Licensed Assault and Rescue Animal'. But one of her spy-dog missions had gone horribly wrong and her orders were clear. *I was to give myself up to the nearest dog rescue shelter and then adopt a family and wait for help. And I couldn't have chosen better,* she smiled, looking around the room at the

Cook children. Ollie had Spud on his knee. The puppy was fast asleep, snoring gently, his chubby tummy breathing in and out. Ollie was the youngest of the children and Lara loved his playfulness. Star and Spud adored him too. Lara watched as Star leapt on to Ollie's lap and snuggled down for an afternoon snooze.

Sophie couldn't help but wander over to her brother and stroke the pups. 'They're sooo cute,' she purred. 'And so squidgy!' Sophie was a true animal lover, destined to become a vet. A chinchilla had been top of her Christmas list for three years running. 'It's a house, not a bloomin' zoo,' was her dad's favourite comment. He always told Sophie she could have a chinchilla if they traded Lara in exchange. He knew there was no way that would ever happen.

Ben was the eldest and therefore the leader. Although Lara was officially the family pet, he regarded her as *his* dog. The pair would spend hours fishing at the canal or playing football in the garden. Star and Spud were a bit young but had begun to practise their headers and volleys. Star could do forty keepie-uppies and Spud had perfected his goal-scoring celebration – a backflip like he'd seen on TV. It was exhausting and they always needed their long afternoon sleeps!

'I think Star will be a good footballer,' Ben told Lara. 'She's got your natural ability.'

Lara looked across at the sleeping Star. She was a tiny puppy with one sticky-up ear just like her mum. She also had the same trademark black and white splodges, including a patch over her eye. She had tiny razor teeth and a very long tongue that sometimes peeped out when she was asleep. *And so clever!*

Lara watched as Spud woke and wandered over to the games console. *Just puppy fat, I'm sure*, she thought, smiling at his low-hanging belly. Spud was bigger than his sister. *Probably because of his liking for custard creams*, thought Lara. A guilty thought passed through her mind. *I wonder where he gets that from!* Spud was a handsome dog, like his father, Potter. Spud had a shiny black coat and a playful puppy face. His ears were a matching pair: floppy, except when he was concentrating or when someone mentioned food. Then he had the biggest ears in the world, pricked and listening for scrapings into his bowl. *Not quite as bright as his sister*, she considered, *although the BrainBox training game is doing him some good.*

Lara was pleased the building work at home had finished. At first she'd been reluctant when the Secret Service had suggested a security upgrade. But Professor Cortex had been very persuasive, arguing that it would allow her to improve the pet neighbourhood watch scheme that she'd set up.

'And now you're a mother,' the professor frowned, 'you have to be extra careful of enemy agents.'

Lara's office was now complete. She pressed the button with her nose and stood in front of the fireplace. *3 . . . 2 . . . 1 . . .*, she counted, and the hearth moved, rotating Lara into her secret office. She sat at the laptop and fixed her spectacles on the end of her nose. Lara took a pencil in her mouth and logged on to her emails. *Nothing particularly exciting*, she thought, although she was pleased to see a message from Professor Cortex confirming tomorrow's visit to Spy School. *Star and Spud will love it*, she thought. *The professor always has oodles of new gadgets and whacky ideas.*

Lara loved the professor. He was a bit grumpy on the outside but a great big softie on the inside. *He was the one who trained me as a spy dog. And who gave me that ridiculous code name, GM451. I am so pleased the family have chosen to call me by my other code name.*

Lara clicked a remote control and various CCTV camera pictures were beamed on to the screen in front of her. She could see most of the neighbourhood from here. The professor's voice replayed in her head. 'You can never be too careful, GM451. You are the cleverest animal in the world. No other animal can understand every human word. Or defuse a bomb. Or play chess, for that matter.' *And he should know*, thought Lara. *He's head of Spy School. And probably the cleverest, maddest scientist in the world.* Lara couldn't quite see where the danger would come from. *After all, this is a quiet road and*

I'm retired from active spy-dog service, she thought. *I can't see that any more baddies are going to come looking for me. But this office is cool*, she admitted, spinning herself round on her leather chair. She cast her mind back over the last year. *Not quite the retirement I'd planned. So many adventures!* Lara shuddered as she remembered falling off a space rocket as it took off, and stopping a diamond robbery. *But being a mum definitely changes things. This time I've given up for real. From now on it's the quiet life for me and the pups.*

Lara watched on CCTV as Mr Granger from number 42 tipped his grass cuttings into next door's garden. *They won't be happy*, she thought. Through another camera she saw a delivery van pull up at number 7. *New sofa*, she noted. *And what a nice pattern.*

Nothing suspicious, she thought. *No sign of baddies.* Lara zoomed in to the van parked outside number 22. *Window cleaner*, she read. *New bloke, by the look of it.* Lara watched for a minute. The man climbed the ladder and she watched with interest as he looked all around before reaching into the upstairs window and climbing in. *Er, I don't think he should be doing that*, she thought, zooming closer still until she could see through the open window. The CCTV showed the window cleaner snooping around the bedroom, putting trinkets into a bag. Suddenly, Lara was on full alert. She looked at her map of the close. *Number 22, Mr and Mrs Winslow. Both teachers. Both out at work all day! Yikes, I think this is a robbery!*

It all started with a Scarecrow.

Puffin is seventy years old.

Sounds ancient, doesn't it? But Puffin has never been
so lively. We're always on the lookout for the next big
idea, which is how it began all those years ago.

Penguin Books was a big idea from the mind of
a man called Allen Lane, who in 1935 invented
the quality paperback and changed the world.
**And from great Penguins, great Puffins grew,
changing the face of children's books forever.**

The first four Puffin Picture Books were hatched in 1940 and the
first Puffin story book featured a man with broomstick arms called
Worzel Gummidge. In 1967 Kaye Webb, Puffin Editor, started the
Puffin Club, promising to **'make children into readers'**.
She kept that promise and over 200,000 children became
devoted Puffineers through their quarterly instalments of
Puffin Post, which is now back for a new generation.

Many years from now, we hope you'll look back and
remember Puffin with a smile. **No matter what your age
or what you're into, there's a Puffin for everyone.**
The possibilities are endless, but one thing is for sure:
whether it's a picture book or a paperback, a sticker book
or a hardback, **if it's got that little Puffin
on it – it's bound to be good.**